The Spanish Medallion

by

Lloyd Peters

Dales Large Print Books
Long Preston, North Yorkshire,
BD23 4ND, England.

British Library Cataloguing in Publication Data.

Peters, Lloyd
The Spanish medallion.

A catalogue record of this book is available from the British Library

ISBN 1-84262-381-8 pbk

First published in Great Britain in 1977 by IPC Magazines Ltd.

Published in Large Print 2005 by arrangement with Lloyd Peters

Dales Large Print is an imprint of Library Magna Books Ltd.

Printed and bound in Great Britain by
T.J. (International) Ltd., Cornwall, PL28 8RW

Chapter One

Mistress Frances Durville peered through her bedroom window into the storm-racked night outside, a night showing no division of sea from sky. She could see nothing except the lightning splitting the blackness occasionally, and almost directly overhead the thunder rolled and vibrated, concentrating its full force, it seemed, on her bedroom.

She was both fascinated and frightened, and remained at the window, the noise of the storm penetrating and continuing to fill her mind with great anxiety regarding her father, Captain Richard Durville. He was in command of the *Frances Anne*, his own merchant ship which, with the *Sea Queen*, also his, had been pressed into the Queen's service to meet the threat of the Spanish Armada. Now he was somewhere out there in that terrible night. Frances prayed fervently that he would come home safely, even if he had to lose his ships.

She remembered how proud he and her mother had been of their first ship, and how they had struggled to make the merchant shipping business grow. Gradually her father had succeeded, and some fifteen years ago the family had gone to live at the small manor house. They had named it Durville Court, and it had been their home ever since.

If only the war was over, Frances thought. For months there had been talk of an invasion, and then about three weeks ago the enemy ships had been sighted. News travelled slowly, and last week in the village she had heard the rumour that the Spaniards were in disarray, their ships dispersed and fleeing into the North Sea.

Suddenly she heard a crash, and felt a tremor run through her bedroom. She listened intently, trying to hear beyond the noise of the wind. For a while she waited silently, but the sound was not repeated.

She opened the door of her bedroom slowly and looked into the semi-darkness of the small gallery. Nothing seemed amiss. Frances stood undecided. What should she do? Should she rouse her mother and Alice, the eldest of their three maid servants, or had they been awakened already? She walked hesitantly along to her mother's door, but there was no sound or movement from within. She retreated into her own bedroom again; it was cold in the gallery.

Frances, her mother, and Alice were alone in that part of the house, but in the small cottage adjoining lived John Standard, her father's right-hand man at Durville Court, and John's wife, Flora. To John Captain Durville had entrusted the safe-keeping of his household when he was away. Frances felt sure that if anything was wrong or danger threatened, John would know about it. Elsewhere in the house were the two young kitchen maids, as well as Jesiah, whose official title was manservant, while outside, in quarters above the stables, lived Casper, the youthful groom. There was also a garrison of soldiers not far away, one of many such dotted about the country, in case the Spaniards attempted a landing on English soil.

Frances opened the curtains of her bedroom window wider, still wondering anxiously about the mysterious noise that had occurred some minutes earlier. Below her window and across the small kitchen garden the ground sloped gradually to a small inlet almost opposite the house. She could now make out the white edging of surf and the darker strip of sand and shingle as the water retreated.

She caught a glimpse of something lying at the water's edge. Leaning forward, still holding on to the curtains, she strained her eyes to see what it was.

Her nose felt the cold of the glass as she pressed her face against the window. Whatever was lying in the inlet was indistinct, and yet there was something about it that was different from other objects that were often thrown up on the shore by the waves.

Then, as she watched, it moved. A moment later she knew that it was a human being. As she looked the figure staggered to its feet, lurched a few yards up the beach and then dropped to its knees and began to crawl until it reached the path.

At this point the man or woman was lost to her sight entirely. Suddenly she glimpsed a movement farther up the winding path. There was the figure again. Her eyes became riveted on it as it stumbled and fell to lie still upon the ground.

Recovering a little from the shock, Frances stepped back from the window. She tried to think of what to do. Help was needed quickly. No good rousing her mother or Alice: by the time they were dressed it might be too late, and she would waste time going for John Standard. She must go herself.

Frances threw on her heavy cloak, picked up her shoes and left her room. Downstairs she saw that the proud, bright, crackling fire of a few hours ago had now settled into a flat, red mass of embers in the grate, giving out a warm, rosy hue around the hearth. She was tempted to linger near it, but only stopped long enough to put her shoes on before making her way to the back door.

Outside the wind rushed at her, and tore at her clothes as if seeking to drive her back inside the house. She ran through the garden and on to the path between the heavy trees leading down to the inlet. Raindrops scattered into her face from overhanging branches, and the cold cut into her. Frances stepped more slowly as she neared the spot where she had seen the figure lying. She stopped and peered apprehensively about her for a moment, and tried to pierce the darkness of the path.

This was no place, she knew, for a young woman to be alone on a stormy night. Supposing whoever it was she had seen on the beach from her window was at that very moment watching her from behind the trees? She wanted to run back to the house now, and yet... She steeled herself and made her way farther down the path, stopping every few yards to peer around her.

Suddenly Frances gasped with shock and stepped back quickly. A man's body lay in front of her, face down and very still, with one arm flung in front of him as if his last movement had been to claw at the earth to pull himself away from the following sea.

She recovered herself a little. Was he dead? Had that been his last movement which she had seen from her bedroom window? Nervously, she moved forward. More to give herself courage than anything else, Frances said: 'Let me help you.' The words sounded foolish, and the wind flung them back. There was no answer from the man, but she had not expected any.

She went nearer, and pulled at the man's shoulder until he rolled loosely on to his back. His dark hair was matted against his face, and she could make out a moustache and small beard in the pale moonlight. The wet material of his clothes clung to his skin, and he breathed with difficulty.

A few moments later Frances had dragged

him off the path and under the shelter of the trees. She rubbed his hands in an effort to revive the man, but he remained inert and limp in the gloom. She sat back on her heels, anxiously biting her lip and staring at him. She could not leave him there, that was certain. If she did, he would die. The man needed warmth quickly, and dry clothes, if he was to be saved.

The rain had now ceased. Frances's home was just discernible against the night sky, and she thought of the fire still red in the grate.

Frances found it difficult to keep a grip on the stranger's wet clothing as she pulled him. But every minute that he remained outside increased the risk to his life. So, stopping only momentarily for breath every now and then, she gradually worked her way up towards the house. Once she sank down at his side, thinking she could not go farther, but then she heard him groan and redoubled her efforts. How far the way seemed to her home! It had never been so far before. At last she reached it and managed to get him inside, and closed the door on the wind and cold. Then, with her remaining strength, she dragged him and laid him down in the calm of the great room, in front of the fading warmth of the fire.

Frances placed more logs on the fire. In a few minutes she knew it would be blazing, throwing out its heat and light on to the unconscious figure lying in front of it.

She hurried unsteadily into the kitchen, and in the darkness found a towel. She returned to the fireside and knelt down and began to wipe the man's face as best she could. She gazed anxiously down as she dried him gently. She saw that he was young. The hair was short and dark, still damp and slightly curled.

She looked at the stranger's unconscious figure. At present he was unlikely to be a trouble to her. No doubt by the time he had come round, the rest of the household would be awake. They could then look after him and find out where he came from, and feed him. She could now hear the man's breathing, and she watched the rise and fall of his chest. Should she go and get John Standard?

Before she could decide anything, her eye was caught by the glint of metal at the man's neck. She bent over him and saw that it was a medallion attached to a thin chain. She took hold of the medallion and held it in the palm of her hand, clear of the stranger's body. It was round, with a cross attached at four points on its inner circumference. In the centre of the cross a man's face was engraved, with lettering below it. It felt weighty, and Frances guessed that it was made of silver. She turned it over in her hand and saw that on the other side a ship instead of a face was engraved. She regarded it with curiosity. There appeared to be an inscription of sorts round the flat rim of that side. She turned it over once again.

Leaning nearer the fire, Frances saw that there was something written beneath the face. Her mouth formed the word slowly. 'Ravallo,' she whispered to herself. It had no meaning for her.

She turned the medallion over again, her eyes strained. There were two words, one above and one below the ship. She did not have to spell them out. She knew immediately!

'Juanita! Armada!' she gasped aloud as the message penetrated her mind.

Frances scrambled instantly to her feet, and retreated quickly some distance away from the stranger, letting the medallion fall back on to his body. A Spaniard! She had brought a Spaniard into her home! An enemy!

Now the firelight showed the tan of his skin. An enemy in Captain Richard Durville's house! The man was unconscious now, but for how long? Her mind was in a turmoil as she stood wide-eyed, hand to lips, fearful of the consequences of what she had done.

After a minute her thoughts steadied, and she approached the Spaniard nervously as if he would suddenly leap up and attack her. She gazed down at the young face. Was this the face of the all-conquering Armada?

One thing was certain, Frances knew. If the stranger was Spanish and the authorities found out, he would be executed immediately. Only if he was an important personage with a ransom would his life be spared. The chances of the man being that were small, she thought as she looked down at him.

She glanced at the clock, its face just visible in the gloom. In about one hour the dawn would come. By then Alice would be stirring. John would be around soon after, and the kitchen would come alive under Flora's hand. What should she do?

Suddenly the Spaniard stirred. His eyelids fluttered and a breath was taken in quickly. Frances, surprised, stepped backwards hastily and nearly fell over a stool behind her. She watched from a distance as his eyelids moved again and remained open.

His head began to turn, and Frances snatched at a sword on the wall and held it nervously in front of her, ready to defend herself. It must be a dream, she thought. She would awake soon in her bed upstairs, the sword would be on the wall in its usual place, the fire would be almost out, and no Spaniard would be lying in front of it.

The man coughed and his body shook a little, and Frances knew that it was no dream. She stood some way beyond his feet where the firelight merged into the shadows, and only her front was visible. Muttered words in another language came from the stranger.

She watched him turn his head from side to side. He was no doubt beginning to think and reason. Soon he would raise his head and see her. His hands moved on the floor, tapping and groping as if searching for something that would tell him where he was. Then slowly and weakly he raised his head, and Frances looked across the fireplace into the conscious face of the man she had brought in from the night.

If she showed alarm, then so did he, turning on to an elbow and recoiling away. At his movement, Frances took an involuntary step backward into the shadow at the foot of the stairs. For a moment they remained as they were, then the man tried to rise from the floor by holding on to a chair; but, still weak from his ordeal, his legs would not hold him and he fell back against the side of the fireplace. There he remained, staring fixedly at Frances.

Frances realised that she was in no immediate danger from the man, and moved forward cautiously into the light again. She saw his eyes widen and drop from her face to stare fixedly at her hands. He tried to hitch himself up taut against the wall. She glanced down. The sword! She was still holding it, and it was pointing directly at the man. By the look on his face, he obviously thought she was going to kill him.

Suddenly his face relaxed, and he regarded Frances calmly and with seeming resignation to his fate. She let the sword hang loosely towards the floor, but remained where she was, looking down on him warily.

The man closed his eyes momentarily, and then looked up at her and said something in a throaty whisper. It was a question, she knew, but it was in Spanish which she did not understand.

She drew nearer to him slowly. She felt she should say something in reply, even if he did not comprehend. She pointed to the window, then said quietly: 'I found you on the beach and brought you here. You are in England.'

There was a slight lightening of the man's expression, but then a weary sadness came over his face as if memories had returned. He reached out an arm as if to touch her, and to her amazement said weakly: 'I thank you, Señorita.'

Frances could hardly believe her ears as she looked into his face. His eyes were dark. She could not see their true colour in the firelight, but in them she saw a returning vitality.

'You speak English?' she gasped in astonishment.

The man nodded and smiled. 'It is of great benefit to speak the language of the country you set out to conquer.' The wryness of the smile took the offence from his words.

'You are a Spaniard?'

'Yes.'

'From the Armada?'

'Yes, a small part – there will not be much left of it.'

'I saw the medallion – I guessed you were.' She indicated his chest where it hung.

A puzzled frown appeared on the Spaniard's face. 'And yet you brought me here?'

'I could not leave you to die, and I did not see the medallion until you were inside,' she replied.

Truth to tell, Frances was very anxious. Time was passing quickly. Her position was one of danger, not only from the Spaniard, but if she was caught giving him shelter the penalty would be severe. She felt sorry for him, enemy though he was. She decided that whatever else happened to him, she would feed him first. She hoped that if ever her father fell into Spanish hands, they would take care of him also.

'Soon it will be daylight,' she said hurriedly. 'I will give you food, and then...' She paused and their eyes met.

The man shook his head. 'No, I am rested. I will go now.' He made to rise, but would have fallen again had not she put out a hand quickly to steady him. She had not meant to get so near to him. She helped him to sit in a chair by the fire.

'You cannot go yet – you are still weak,' said Frances.

Her companion nodded. 'You are right, I have been many days with little to eat.' He glanced at the sword still in her hand. 'You may put your weapon down, Señorita. You are in no danger from me, I promise you.'

For the first time that night Frances smiled – a little, tired smile. She must look rather foolish clutching the sword, and yet she could not be sure of what he may do if she were without it. 'Do not move from the chair,' she said firmly. 'If you do, I will shout. My father and brother are upstairs,' she lied.

Still carrying the sword, she left him and hurried across to the kitchen. A pan of porridge was cooking at the back of the fire. Frances lifted it on to the hot coals. When it was ready, she saw that he was shivering, and his hands were unsteady. She laid the sword on the hearth, and proceeded to feed him spoonful by spoonful, glancing occasionally towards the stairs in case they had been heard. What the Spaniard thought of English porridge he did not say, but he took each mouthful hungrily. Once, in her hurry, she must have forced too much into his mouth, and he drew back sharply. Concern sprang into her face. 'Sorry,' she muttered.

The Spaniard shook his head slightly, and a hand came up and touched her sleeve. From that moment Frances felt that the tension that had existed between them since the stranger had regained consciousness was gone.

As she fed him, she noted the lines of fatigue in the young, lean face. It was a proud, determined, and sensitive face, nevertheless. Enemy though he was, Frances could not bring herself to allow him to go until his condition had improved.

An idea was forming in her mind. Why

should she not hide him for another day? After all, one young survivor from the Armada was not going to pose a threat to England, if the Armada itself had failed against it. Then, when he had slept and was stronger, he would have a better chance of getting back to Spain and home. A small chance, but the alternative was death if he was caught on English soil.

'You must not go yet,' she said. 'You are shivering, and your clothes are still wet. You can hide here. I will find a place for you.'

He shook his head and looked up at her from the chair. 'No! Many thanks, Señorita, but I must go.' He began to raise himself out of the chair.

'Come closer to the fire and warm yourself first, then,' she said, supporting him as he rose to his feet for the first time. With her assistance he walked unsteadily until they were both staring into the heart of the fire. Steam rose from his clothes.

'What are you going to do? Where will you hide?' asked Frances in a low, urgent voice.

'I do not know. Perhaps I will find some of my friends. Some may have got ashore. Then together we shall try to get across the Channel to Antwerp, and…'

'Antwerp!' exclaimed Frances incredulously. She glanced anxiously over her shoulder and put a hand to her lips on forgetting to speak softly. She heard nothing. 'But that is hundreds of miles away,' she went on. 'You will not get one mile from here before you are caught.' She turned to face her companion. 'Look at you. No shoes, no jerkin or cloak. Though it is not winter, you would surely die before long. You need more rest.'

He drew himself away from the stone of the fireplace. 'Perhaps, Señorita, it is better that way than to hang at the hands of your countrymen.'

Frances pushed her hair back in an angry gesture, and her eyes flashed. 'Better I had left you to die on the beach.'

The Spaniard's dark face showed surprise, and then concern. 'Let us not quarrel. I owe you my life.'

'Yes, and how long will you keep it if you leave now?'

It suddenly occurred to her how strange the conversation was. England and Spain were at war, and here was she, the daughter of an English captain, trying to prevent a Spaniard from killing himself!

Something of the same idea must have struck her companion, for he said: 'Do you forget that I am an enemy?'

Frances regarded him, and saw in his eyes a glint of humour that took away some of the seriousness of his words. She shook her head. 'No, but on the beach you were not. You were someone needing help. You still need help,' she added simply.

He looked into the fire for a few moments, then turned to her again, and his face was serious in the extreme. 'You understand,' he said quietly, 'the danger to you and your family if I am found here. It is better that I go now.'

'Then the risk that I ran to get you here was for nothing,' stated Frances in a resigned fashion. She went on: 'I know that you will not be alive tomorrow night if you leave now.'

There was silence between them. Outside, in the front of the house, the trees rustled in the dying wind. 'It is true,' said the stranger, 'that the battle is over for me.'

'I know where you could hide,' said Frances hurriedly. 'In the schoolroom upstairs. It's never used now. There is a bed, you would be safe. I will find clothes for you, and then tomorrow, at night, you will have the darkness to protect you.'

Her companion considered a moment, and then nodded in agreement. 'Then I will stay, but I am frightened for you.'

She smiled, shaking her head. 'No one will know.'

The concern in his face gave way to a grateful smile. 'I do not understand the English. You risk death to help an enemy.'

'If I were your sister, I would wish that someone would help you when you were in need,' she said. 'You must come quickly. You have little time,' she whispered, and began to move towards the stairs.

Frances half-supported the Spaniard as they climbed the stairs and crossed the passage. She opened the door to the empty schoolroom, and with a great sigh of relief ushered him inside. It was cold there. 'Wait! I will bring clothes and blankets.'

Within five minutes a candle flickered in the draught, illuminating the old schoolroom. In a corner was a truckle bed piled with assorted coverings, anything that she had been able to lay her hands on from her own bedroom.

'Tomorrow,' she said in a hushed voice, 'I will light a fire in here for you. I will say that I am going to clean the room out. Nobody will suspect.' She went towards the door, then looked back. 'I will bring you food and drink when I can.' With that she slipped out and locked the door from the outside, and crept downstairs, thinking how dreadfully tired she was now.

The sword lay in the hearth. She picked it

up and replaced it on the wall. It would not do if that, or anything else, was found out of place.

When Frances awoke it was to the sound of excited voices outside her bedroom door. Sudden fear made her sit up in her bed. The Spaniard! Had he been discovered? She crept to the door, her heart beating fast. She could hear Alice's high-pitched tones and her mother's calmer voice. The talk seemed to be concerning trees. Bewildered, Frances wrapped a gown around her and slipped into the gallery.

The two people who had been staring through the gallery window now turned quickly when they heard her door open.

'Mistress Frances! Look! The tree's blown down.' The maid pointed outside.

A surge of relief went through Frances that the Spaniard was still hidden, followed by astonishment as she gazed between Alice and her mother into the front garden below.

A tree had indeed fallen, one of a group of four, one at each corner of the ornamental garden. It lay across a flattened hedge and flowerbeds, its upper branches almost touching the foot of another.

Frances realised then that the noise she had heard during the night had been the tree crashing to earth. Had it not kept her awake, she would not have seen the Spaniard on the beach. She could not help glancing quickly in the direction of the door behind which the stranger was hiding as she turned away from the window. As soon as she got a chance, she would see how he was faring.

'Good morning, Frances,' said Mrs Durville, putting a hand to her forehead and closing her eyes momentarily. 'I thought the end of us had come. What a storm came over last night! I dared not move. I prayed for all here, and that your father would be in safe anchorage away from the Spaniards and the sea.'

Frances hastened to reassure her mother. 'The Spaniards have gone, Mother – their ships have foundered,' she said firmly. Mrs Durville looked slightly surprised at her daughter's words, uttered so confidently. Seeing this, Frances added quickly: 'That wind will have driven them back to Spain, I am sure.' She realised she would have to guard her tongue from now on. She added: 'And Father will be on his way back at this moment, without doubt.'

'I hope so, I do hope so,' said her mother anxiously.

While wanting her father back safely, Frances wished fervently that he would not arrive before nightfall. She wanted time to sort out the problem of the Spanish survivor. Her father's return early that day would complicate matters.

'I do not wish to live to hear another storm like that,' Mrs Durville said. 'The house was alive – knocks and bangs and suchlike.'

Alice tugged at her cap with both hands. 'It was full of demons last night, mistress, I can tell you. I swear that I heard voices in the wind.'

Frances smiled inwardly. If Alice only knew whose the voices in the wind were!

She said cheerfully: 'But, Alice, look at the day it has bred, how beautiful it is now.'

Mrs Durville made a gesture towards the stairs. 'Your work during the day will perhaps drive out those thoughts of yours, Alice.'

Alice gave a sniff, and left them to clomp down the steps, muttering loudly: 'It were no good spirit that brought the tree down.'

As the maid and her forebodings faded from sight and sound, Mrs Durville turned back to Frances. 'A silly woman's tale – don't let it upset you, Frances.'

She shook her head. 'It is of no matter, I have heard her stories before.'

Mrs Durville regarded her daughter, the blush of pink in the clear skin under the long, fair hair falling to rounded shoulders. Graceful and worthy of the noblest male hand in the land, she thought. An independent girl and kind. A beautiful girl – nay a woman now, and all of twenty-two. 'Did the storm keep you awake, Frances?' she asked, noting the dark circles under her daughter's eyes.

'I awakened once or twice, Mother, that was all,' she replied. She felt on edge. Her mother stood not ten feet away from the old schoolroom door, and besides, Frances was impatient to find out how the Spaniard was.

'Is anything wrong, Frances?' enquired her mother, searching her daughter's face.

She gave a quick shake of the head. She glanced at her mother and away again. 'I have a slight headache, perhaps from the storm.' She shrugged and turned towards her own door.

Mrs Durville looked after her daughter anxiously. If only she would marry and settle down, she thought. Always there was some excuse whenever young men showed interest. There had been numerous proposals of marriage, but whenever Mrs Durville had taxed her over the matter, her daughter's answer had been the same. She had liked the suitor well enough, but she did not love him. And that was that! Mrs Durville despaired.

'Have you breakfasted yet, Mother?' Frances asked suddenly.

'No, you know what I am like about eating early in the day.' She paused, then added: 'Though I think it's past the hour of ten.'

'I shall breakfast in my room,' said Frances, 'then rest a while. Would you ask Alice to bring it up?'

Mrs Durville looked worried. She moved away, saying over her shoulder: 'I will tell Alice, then I must make preparation for your father's homecoming. He may be home today, and I must be ready.'

Frances returned to her room and looked out of her window. There was the small bay, gentler waves now breaking on to its sloping shore. The trees near the path were drying out under the morning sun, and beyond everything the sea placidly twinkled and swelled gently in a satisfied way after the violence of the night.

On any ordinary day she would have been taking a walk past the bay and along the strip of sand which ran for a mile or two, broken only by other bays, some of shingle, some of sand, white beneath the feet, others of boulders and rocks. She knew them all well. Hearts Point, Sunset Bay, Honest Bay, Levers Head. Beyond and farther up the coast the rocks were like teeth, the headlands large and overhanging, the currents and winds dangerous.

Frances left the window, her thoughts returning to the stranger next door. It was difficult for her to think of anything else. She sat down at her dressing table and set about making herself look presentable for her next meeting with him.

A knock at the door disturbed her thoughts and Alice appeared, carrying the breakfast tray. Hardy had she set the tray down before she said: 'Flora's found a pan – it's had porridge in it! She swears she left her kitchen tidy last night. She cannot understand it!'

Frances turned away to hide her expression from Alice. The pan! She had forgotten about it! She thought quickly. Better to allay any suspicion before it built up in people's minds. 'You may put Flora's mind at rest, Alice,' she said. 'I couldn't sleep. I went downstairs.'

Alice put her hand to her almost non-existent bosom and a look of relief passed over her mobile features. 'Oh, Mistress Frances, and me thinking that...'

Frances gave a quick smile as she interrupted. 'I know, you thought a demon took porridge in Durville Court!' She wanted Alice out of the way and downstairs quickly. She ushered her to the door. 'Now tell Flora that all is well.' Then she watched as the maid went down the stairs hurriedly.

Alone again, Frances glanced at the tray. Porridge! The poor fellow! Still, it was food, and that was what he needed. Cautiously she opened her door and listened. Voices from below – that was all. She slipped from her room and crept to the old schoolroom door. She knocked, inserted the key, turned it, and after a quick glance along the passage, pushed the door open and entered with some degree of nervousness.

The Spaniard was outlined against the window with his back to it. Frances could not see his face clearly, and she remained near the door, holding the tray.

'Good morning,' she said quietly, 'here is food for you – porridge again.' She smiled apologetically. 'You will think that we English eat nothing else.'

He moved away from the window and came towards her. For a moment she felt afraid. Had she been foolish in entering the room?

He said quietly: 'Good morning. A prisoner cannot choose, Señorita.'

Frances gave an audible sigh of relief. She saw his slow smile, tiny at first, and broadening into a show of teeth. She was to come to know this characteristic well.

She saw that he was wearing some of her father's old clothes which had been amongst those she had gathered hastily together the night before. The garments were ill-fitting, her father being a shorter man and of rounder build, but despite this rather comical aspect, the Spaniard stood before Frances with an air of quiet authority about him.

She set the tray down on a stool. 'Have you fared well?' she asked.

He nodded. 'I feel better. My thanks to you. But your northern seas must have entered my blood. I shiver even though the sun shines.'

'I shall make a fire in here for you.'

The Spaniard shook his head. 'No, you have done enough.' He glanced at the food. 'When I have eaten I shall be warm.'

Frances moved towards the door. 'I will leave you, and…'

'No!' His hand reached out to her. 'Stay, please. I would talk with you.'

She tried the door to make sure she had locked it, then returned to sit down opposite him.

The Spaniard ate all the porridge hungrily before he put the dish down. He glanced towards the window. 'Today it is warm and sunny. How different in the night. I cannot remember much after the *Juanita* went down.'

'What happened?' asked Frances with

great interest.

'Most of the ships were separated in the storm,' he explained. 'We and the *San Miguel* made for a bay. We could see little. My ship hit a rock. It went down suddenly.' He bowed his head and shook it sadly. 'My poor friends.' He was silent at the memory for a moment, then continued in a whisper: 'The water came over me. Huge, black water. Round and round...' He broke off and shrugged, then took a drink of the milk that Frances had brought.

'And then you found yourself in my house.'

The Spaniard nodded, then glanced sideways at her with a glint of amusement in his eyes and continued to regard her. 'Yes, I awoke. I feel the warmth – I see light. I do not know where I am. Then an angel with golden hair is near to me.'

A touch of pink brushed Frances's cheeks at his words. Anyone looking less like an angel on that occasion she could not imagine, being wet, weary and bedraggled.

He raised his eyes to the ceiling and then

looked back again to her. 'But then, this angel became a woman with a sword. I do not know what is happening. I do not understand. If I am to die, that is Fate. But at the hands of a woman!'

Frances began to laugh, then stopped suddenly, hand to mouth, and listened. She went to the door, put her ear to it. But all she could hear were the muted voices from below.

She returned to her seat and smiled rather shamefacedly at the man opposite, and she resumed their quiet conversation. 'I was frightened, too – I did not know what you would do. My scramble to get the sword was very undignified.'

The Spaniard regarded her for a moment reflectively, then shook his head very slowly. The eyes held hers and were serious. 'I shall remember how you looked all my life.'

There was silence between them. It was a compliment, she knew. She lowered her gaze before his, then stood up and wandered over to the window. 'You must stay until dark, until everyone is asleep.'

The Spaniard rose to his feet and joined her, the smile in his eyes again. 'Yes, if you will tell me one thing?'

She turned to face him. 'If I can.'

'Your name,' her companion said gently.

In the light from the window Frances observed the young Spaniard's dark skin, the small beard and moustache. When she talked to this man she seemed to be in a world apart from her everyday one, as if he and she were alone in the only house in the world.

'Frances,' she answered. 'Frances Durville.'

The Spaniard's eyes widened. 'Frances! Francesca! Ah! You have almost a Spanish name, Francesca in my country. It is Fate. I am saved far from home by a girl called Francesca. I have eaten and slept under your roof, Francesca. It is time that I gave you my name also. I am Don Pedro de Ravallo.' He took Frances's hand and bowed over it, then lifted smiling eyes to hers, and in soft accented tones said: 'I was a soldier of King Felipe. Now I am prisoner and captive of Señorita Frances Durville.'

She inclined her head, then returned his look. 'But not for long, Don Pedro de Ravallo.' She caught sight of Flora in the garden below, and drew Pedro away from the window quickly, saying: 'If you are seen, you will be a prisoner of the English authorities.'

His face had tautened, the smile had gone. 'There is someone there?'

'Flora, the cook.' Frances saw the strain in Pedro's face, and she hastened to reassure him: 'She did not see you.'

He looked relieved, then said: 'For a moment when we talked I forgot, Frances, that our countries are at war. Though I have fear for you, if you are caught with me. I am a soldier. If I am caught it is war, but you…'

'There is little danger, Pedro, for me,' she replied. All the same, she knew she had better show herself downstairs soon. It was no good inviting suspicion. 'I must go now,' she told him, 'and you must rest if you are to escape the soldiers tonight.'

As Frances dressed back in her own

bedroom she thought about the man she had just left. She had been right from the first: he was no common soldier that she had brought into the house. She wondered if he would ever see Spain and his family again. Tomorrow he would be gone, one young man fleeing an alien country, arriving one night, disappearing in the darkness of another. But as she walked downstairs that morning, one fragment of her mind, not yet ordered into conscious thought, was hoping that the handsome Spaniard would, by some miracle, stay a little longer.

Chapter Two

Downstairs, Frances found Flora busy in her kitchen. She was a large, finely built woman with grey, kindly eyes, not quite matching the colour of her hair. She looked up as Frances entered, straightened her back and smoothed her apron.

'Morning, Mistress Frances,' said Flora, blowing out her full cheeks.

'Morning, Flora. How fine it is after the storm.'

Flora glanced out of the window. Seagulls wheeled and screamed in delight in the sun again. ''Tis fine now,' she said, 'but I cannot bring to memory such a bad summer. I've shivered and bent before it.' She shrugged and continued, emotion coming into her voice: 'P'raps good weather will stay now, if Sir Frances has scattered the Spanish devils!'

Frances could not help laughing inwardly, and wondered what Pedro would think of Flora's calling him a 'Spanish devil', and her reaction if she knew one of them was upstairs, a guest at Durville Court.

Flora put a loaf to bake, stirred the contents of the pot over the fire, and then took hold of a dish full of fruit and emptied its contents on to the table. She began to slice them, and a puzzled frown appeared on her face. She shook her head slowly as if at some private memory and said: 'Mistress Frances, my eyes are old and given to playing tricks, but when I was in the garden I would swear that a man stood in the window upstairs.'

'A man!' Frances tried to sound surprised.

Flora patted her bosom. 'I sat meself down, the strength left me.'

'We're all tired, Flora,' Frances said quickly. 'The storm put fear into us all. Weary eyes can play tricks, and all this talk these months of the Armada coming. We are fit to imagine anything.'

Flora nodded, and a more settled look came over her features at Frances's words.

It was two hours later before Frances managed to smuggle more food to Pedro. This time she took a plateful of mutton and a large slice of apple tart. He ate the lot with relish, and Flora would have been pleased by his praise of her cooking had Frances been able to tell her.

It had been a difficult journey from the dining table to the old schoolroom. The fact that Mrs Durville's appetite was blunted by excitement at the expected homecoming of her husband helped Frances, Mrs Durville leaving the table early to see that beer and other drinks were in plentiful supply, and to supervise the cleaning and polishing of the best silver and pewter plate that would grace the celebration table when Captain Durville returned.

For a while they talked quietly together, Frances remembering to tell Pedro that Flora had seen him at the window and that he must be more careful. She found out that he was one year older than herself, and she expressed slight surprise to find out that he was a soldier and not a sailor.

Pedro smiled wryly, saying: 'If we had more sailors instead of being mostly soldiers, we may have fared better against the English.' Then he went on to say that early in the battle the English ships, being easier to handle, had harried the Spanish ships, and had kept the wind behind them all the way up the Channel.

They were beset by storms all the way, and

Frances saw the anguish on Pedro's face at the memory. He finished by telling her that he doubted there was a noble house in all Spain that had not lost a son or father in the Armada. All Spain would be in mourning if the rest of the ships had gone down.

'But you are saved, Pedro,' she said, consolingly.

'Yes, I am saved, by the courage of an Englishwoman. If I reach Spain again, King Felipe will be the first to hear of what you did for me.'

Suddenly anger rose in Frances at the mention of the Spanish King. Was he not responsible for her father being away and for the poor souls drowned or smashed upon the rocks through his greedy and seemingly ill-fated venture against England?

'A fig for your King Felipe!' she blurted out, hardly able to keep her voice down. 'I have no sorrow or thoughts for your master. Did he think that Queen Elizabeth would bow the knee to him!'

Her eyes flashed, and Pedro de Ravallo was

taken aback at this sudden outburst. Then he stood up quickly, his face suddenly taut, the large brown eyes bleak in their look.

'Your captains,' he said, his voice tight with suppressed emotion, 'have plundered our ships and ports for too long.'

'Yes,' retorted Frances, standing to face him, 'ships full of stolen treasure, and Spain made rich with your sacking of the Americas.' She drew breath quickly and went on: 'Why should we not take from you that which is not yours?'

He swallowed and swept the room with his arms. 'Then you do not mind being in this fine house, no doubt built with money that is not yours?'

Upset, she moved toward the door. 'My father does not get a living from invading other countries,' she flung at Pedro de Ravallo. 'But this time I hope he does sack a Spanish ship – the spoils will be his from an enemy attacking our country. I shall welcome them.' Frances opened the door and then slammed it behind her without thinking, and made her way downstairs in an agitated frame of mind.

Passing through the hall, Frances met John Standard. Well past middle-age, he was, but still fit and strong, except for his left arm, which was withered and almost useless – the result of being hit with a musket ball in a raid on a Spanish port some years before.

Frances smiled fondly at him. 'Good day to you, John.' She couldn't help noticing the air of suppressed excitement about him. 'I was troubled to see the tree had spoiled your garden with its falling, and after all your labours in it.'

'It's a pity, Mistress Frances,' and here a note of triumph came into his voice, 'but the wind that blew the tree down blew the Spanish ships on to the rocks last night. I saw Parson Critty in the village this morning, and he says that one went down in Dog Bay, and the other is still afloat in Levers Bay, and…'

'Still afloat?' Frances exclaimed in great surprise.

'Aye, but that's not the end of it, Mistress

Frances. The Dons have come ashore and taken over Levers Castle.'

Levers Castle was an abandoned fortress some two miles up the coast. It had been empty some years. Parts of it were crumbling, but a section of it was habitable.

John spoke again. 'A messenger's gone from the village to the garrison, but it will be some hours before the soldiers arrive. I was hastening to bring warning to you and Mistress Durville not to go outside. I'll bolt all the doors, Mistress Frances.' He began to move away, but, seeing the worried look on her face, stopped and said: 'I've a mind to think, Mistress Frances, that the Dons are holding the fort until the ship's repaired, then they'll bolt for Spain.'

She felt somewhat relieved at his words. His supposition was a sensible one. A small force, even well-armed, was not going to stay on enemy territory any longer than they could help once their ship was repaired.

John went off to find Casper and Jesiah, to alert them to the possible danger, leaving

Frances for the moment undecided as to what she should do next – find her mother, or inform Pedro de Ravallo that some Spanish soldiers and a ship were near at hand? She decided on the former. A few minutes spent looking for her mother would make no difference to him. It would also be foolish for him to leave during daylight, but he could set out as soon as it was dark to join up with his countrymen.

She found her mother in the still-room checking on the quantity of ale there. She imparted the news. Mrs Durville received it calmly, but her face grew serious.

'We shall have to prepare ourselves. Tell the men to keep arms by them, Frances. I will gather the women together.'

Frances watched as her mother left the still-room, then crossed the hall quickly and mounted the stairs as fast as her skirts would allow her. How pleased Pedro would be at the news she was bringing. She would apologise for her ill-mannered outburst. No one was about, the gallery was empty.

She reached the old schoolroom door. The key to it! Where was it? She felt about her person hastily. She could not find it. She tried the door. To her surprise it opened. She must have forgotten to lock it earlier. She slipped in, shutting the door quickly, and then turned into the room, expecting to see Pedro de Ravallo.

But her Spanish visitor had gone. The room was empty! So was the tiny room off it. She called softly, thinking he may have thought it was someone else and hidden. No answer. She realised how foolish she was – there was nowhere for him to hide. But where had he gone?

She leaned against the door behind her, and remembered her conversation with John in the hall near the steps, no doubt overheard by Pedro de Ravallo. It was clear to her what had happened then. She had spoken to her mother in the still-room, John had gone off to find the others. The Spaniard must have taken his chance and slipped out unnoticed.

Frances felt sad. She did not blame him

for leaving as he had; she hoped that he would reach the ship safely in time to join it, but she was sorry that they had parted on a note of anger.

The next day near noon a ship was sighted to the north and standing out to sea. Casper's young eyes saw it first. John, squinting at it through the window, thought it was a Spaniard, but was not sure.

Then came the sound of knocking at the front door. A hush fell on everyone present. John went to answer it. They heard him open the door and a voice came clearly:

'Tell your master the Spaniards have gone – the ship has sailed.' It was a messenger from Colston Hall.

Later that afternoon Frances's father returned, the sound of a horse ridden hard heralding his approach. Alice glimpsed him first from the parlour window. Her voice rang excitedly as she dashed into the hall. 'The master's back! The master's back!'

Frances and her mother, busy upstairs sorting out some linen, looked at each other in joyous surprise and hurried downstairs together.

Captain Richard Durville stood in the doorway, his arms flung wide in a happy anticipation of the welcome to come. He embraced first his wife, then his daughter. 'My dear wife, Marion. Frances, my child.'

Frances flung herself against her father for a moment. She kissed him on the cheek, then drew away, but could not conceal the few tears. 'You are safe, Father.'

He nodded, glancing from one to the other and putting an arm around each. He smiled. 'How good is my welcome home.'

'You will be hungry, Richard,' said Mrs Durville. 'If I had known you were to come this hour, I would have had food ready.'

'No matter, Marion,' said her husband, 'I shall eat well when it is. In the meantime, I am glad to be here with you.'

'Is it true, then, that we have won a great victory?' asked Mrs Durville of her husband.

Captain Durville's face lost its tired expression for a moment. 'A great victory,' he said emphatically. 'Never have I seen such handling of fighting ships.'

'Then all is well,' said Mrs Durville, smiling contentedly up into her husband's face.

'It is, Marion, my wife,' replied he, clasping both her hands in a comforting gesture in his own. 'Now that the Armada is defeated and Queen Bess has finished with the hire of our ships, we can return to peaceful business. Our ships shall trade again.'

That evening a celebration in honour of Captain Durville's homecoming was held. Tables were placed end to end in the hall; everybody lent a hand, and before long it was hard to see the white of the tablecloths, so many dishes of different kinds of food were there! Everyone of the household was present, and the banquet was a great success. The wine and ale flowed freely, and soon the hall was filled with the chatter of voices, clinking of glasses, and the splashing of wine.

Many were the questions asked of Captain Durville regarding his adventures against the Armada, and Frances noticed that at each separate telling the Spanish ships got larger, more numerous, and more fearsome.

It was well past midnight before the hall, scene of the welcome home to Captain Durville, was quiet again. Only the shadows cast by the fire moved upon the walls, and even they were tiny as the flames began to die away.

In her room Frances undressed wearily. The excitement and incidents of the day seemed to have left her nearly drained of energy. She blew out the candles and glanced out of the window. It was dark with no moon, but fine and calm. She sighed as she got into bed. Somewhere out there, and by now far away, was Pedro de Ravallo. Survivor of the defeated Spanish Armada he may be, but she knew that he had already stolen, in the short time he had been on English soil, a piece of her heart.

Tomorrow, if it was fine, she would go for a brisk walk or a ride along the beach. The last day or two she had been in the house too much. She yawned and eased her head on the pillow.

A sound came from behind her. Frances's eyes widened in the darkness. What was that? She lifted her head slightly, listening acutely. It came again a few seconds later. Something striking the window. She turned towards it, staring and waiting. Again! The impact against the glass made her draw back involuntarily, the sound sharp in the stillness of the night. She eased herself out of bed slowly, breathing shallowly.

Frances moved carefully to the window and looked out. At first she could see nothing directly below, but then she discerned a movement nearer the kitchen garden. Someone was down there, trying to attract her attention. She moved cautiously to the middle window. It was stiff to open, inch by inch, the night air entering through the gap. She leaned forward as she pushed and gazed down nervously, her fair hair escaping through the window.

The blur of a face looking up and a hand which waved, riveted her attention. But the hoarsely-whispered name which she heard made her senses reel. Ravallo! Pedro de Ravallo! The shock made her incapable of moving for the moment, then she recovered sufficiently to stand upright away from the window. It was not true. How could it be?

'Francesca,' whispered the figure.

Joy followed the shock. 'Wait, Pedro!' she flung down through the opening to him. Sharply awake now, her heart beating fast, Frances threw on her cloak, pushed her feet into her slippers and hastened, treading softly, downstairs. She knew that danger to the Spaniard was even more acute this time than on his first arrival. Now that her father was home the enemy would receive short shrift if found in his house!

It was dark in the passage, and she groped her way to the back door. 'Pedro, it is Frances,' she whispered. There was a sound from the other side of the door.

'Francesca,' came Pedro de Ravallo's hushed voice from a few inches away. His tone sounded thankful and relieved.

'Are you alone, Pedro?'

'Yes, do not be afraid, Frances.' There was a moment's silence, then he added with grim humour: 'I think I am the only live Spaniard left in England.'

She turned the key and pulled the door open slowly. The shadowy figure of Don Pedro de Ravallo stood alone in the doorway. She could hardly see his features.

'I did not mean to frighten you, Frances,' he whispered urgently. 'I have nowhere else to go. I thought of you.' He slipped into the passage beside her, and she closed the door very carefully after him, hardly conscious of his words and still recovering from the shock of his reappearance.

'But the ship. I saw…'

Her companion's voice came out of the darkness close by. 'I did not reach it in time, Frances. The *San Miguel* had put to sea. I ran, but I was too late. Then the English soldiers came. I had to hide among the rocks until nightfall. It has taken a long time returning.'

'But you are safe again, Pedro.'

'Yes, for now, Francesca.' She noticed how he slipped occasionally into the Spanish version of her name. It sounded beautiful the way he pronounced it.

'What will you do now?' she asked anxiously.

He sighed, then said thoughtfully: 'Perhaps it would be best if I tried to gain Plymouth.'

'No!' exclaimed Frances in a heavy whisper. 'No! The port will be full of English ships. That is Drake's harbour. My father has just returned from there, you would have no chance.'

'Your father? But I thought...'

'Yes, I told you he was here. I was frightened then. I did not know you.'

'And now?' There was the hint of a smile in his voice.

'I think you are an honourable man.'

There was silence between them for a moment in the blackness of the passage, then the Spaniard said: 'And an unmannerly one, Francesca. I was a guest in your house.

I provoked you, and then I left without giving thanks to you.'

'It does not matter, Pedro, we must not quarrel again. I am thankful you are safe,' said Frances, and then added: 'But for how long?'

'I will travel at night – keep to the woods and fields.'

'No! Stay here again, Pedro.'

'I cannot, Francesca, it is too dangerous, and now that your father is returned it is more so.'

In her heart she knew that what he said was true. She had hidden him once for a short while successfully, but another time there might be dire consequences. 'Yes, you are right,' she admitted sadly. 'But you must eat before you go. This way,' she whispered, searching and finding his sleeve in the darkness. Then they crept along the passage to the door leading to the hall. She opened it and waited, her senses keenly alert, and hoping that the large amounts of wine and ale consumed by the rest of the household would keep them asleep for the rest of the night!

In the dim light from the fire the tablecloth showed ghostly white, with lifeless candlesticks standing among the dirty plates and glasses, just as they had been left after the celebration a few hours before. The smell of wine and beer lingered in the warm air. Frances knew that there was plenty of food left untouched.

'Warm yourself,' she whispered, 'while I get you food.' She saw his eyes widen at the sight of the table before he went to stand near the fire.

Fearful of making a sound, Frances hastily gathered as much food as she could carry. Then it was with great relief that she followed Pedro back into the passage and its enveloping and protective darkness again.

While her visitor ate hungrily, Frances said: 'You must take great care on your journey, Pedro.'

'I shall remember, Francesca, that you saved my life and helped me when I was alone. I shall not throw that life away easily.'

He paused, then continued: 'Our countries are still at war, Francesca, but when I return to Spain I will find some way of repaying you for your bravery.' Then there was laughter in his hushed tones as he added: 'I shall have a ship deliver a chest full of jewels to you on the path where you found me.'

Frances, moved by his words, reached out and touched him, a light, private gesture, instinctive and coming before her words. 'When I found you, you were somebody needing help; you still need help. I shall never think of you as an enemy, Pedro.' She heard him sigh in the darkness.

'When there is peace, I shall come and see you, Frances. We shall talk openly together.'

'I would like that,' she replied softly.

There was silence for a few moments between them, and Frances wished she could see his face. Then Pedro spoke again.

'I have troubled you long enough, Frances. Now I shall go while it is still dark. There will be no more danger for you.'

'But great danger for you, Pedro. I fear for

your life,' she said, her voice carrying the great anxiety she felt. 'How far can you travel on foot before dawn?' she asked. Before he could speak she answered the question herself. 'It will not be many miles, and then...'

'There is nothing else that I can do, Frances,' he said calmly. 'I must take the chance.'

She heard him move towards the door. 'Wait, Pedro!' she exclaimed urgently. 'I have thought. Take one of the horses. Mine, Bluebell. She will carry you far. I will say she wandered away.'

He hesitated for a moment, and when he spoke his voice was low. 'Of all the houses in England, I find help in the one where an angel dwells. My debt to you will be unpayable.'

'It is of no account, Pedro. I would only ask of you that you will let me know by some means that you are safe.'

'I will find a way, Francesca,' he replied firmly.

'Then quickly,' she said, pushing past him and opening the door. 'You must be careful,

Pedro. Casper sleeps above the stable. I will rouse Bluebell and bring her out to you.'

Silently the figures of Frances and Don Pedro de Ravallo stole along the outside of the house to the stable. When they had almost reached it, Pedro stopped to face her. 'I will leave you here, Frances,' he said. 'If this Casper sees us together, there will be danger for you.'

'No, it is better that I come,' she replied. 'The horse knows me. We shall not be seen.' Frances, her eyes now accustomed to the dark after the blackness of the passage, discerned a look of exasperation on the Spaniard's face.

'Very well, but I must say farewell here, Francesca. There will be no time in there.' He reached for her hand and bent low over it. His lips pressed hard against it.

The next moment he had turned away, and she tiptoed ahead quickly to the stable. But if Francesca was light-footed at that moment, her heart was heavy with her sadness at Pedro's going. Only now had she become fully aware of her real feelings towards him.

She stood just inside the entrance and listened intently, and heard the rustling of straw as one of the horses moved on scenting her presence. She hoped that Casper was fast asleep under the influence of the ale he had drunk.

Bluebell stirred at her mistress's approach. 'Bluebell, girl,' breathed Frances, 'Bluebell.' As she bent over the animal she realised that it was probably the last time she would see it. It would be a miracle if the horse found its way home again.

Bluebell got to her feet, and Frances, her heart pounding in her ears, began to lead the horse gently towards the entrance. Its feet stirring the straw and dirt sounded loud in the stillness. She prayed that Casper would remain in the loft, unconscious of what was going on below.

But he must have heard something. Suddenly there was the blur of a face at the top of the loft steps, a tremulous voice. 'Wh-who's there?'

Frances, rooted to the spot with the sudden shock for a moment, recovered her wits and pushed Bluebell at Pedro. He flung himself on to her back, and for a moment was side-on to Frances. A quick movement of his hand, and something was pushed into hers. Then, seconds later, Don Pedro de Ravallo was racing away down the drive and away over the fields into the night.

Frances turned and ran the opposite way, hoping that she had not been seen. She gained her back door again, entered it and flew along the passage and up the stairs into the welcome safety of her bedroom. There she flung herself down on the bed, the linen becoming wet with tears of unhappiness. The man who had entered her life in such a strange fashion had now left it, probably to go to his death. Her hand was closed tightly around the medallion and chain which he had worn, and then given to her at the last moment before his escape.

In a short time candlelight showed under her door. She heard footsteps and doors opening, her father's voice and John's, then Casper's. She put her ear to the door.

'It's Bluebell, Mistress Frances's horse, master, that's gone,' Casper was saying. 'Fast asleep I was. It galloped like the wind. Two or more of 'em.'

'Did you see the rogues?' came her father's voice.

'No,' came the reply to Frances's relief. 'Too dark, master.'

'All right,' said her father, 'go with John and Jesiah and search the grounds, though I fear you will find nought of them.' There was a pause, and then she heard her father continue: 'A man does not steal a horse at this time of the night and then wait for someone to catch him!'

And of course Captain Durville was quite right, as Frances knew he would be. A search of the grounds of the house revealed no trace of anyone, and after Jesiah had been detailed to keep watch in the stables with a somewhat nervous Casper, the house quietened again.

Chapter Three

The next morning, after a half-hearted attack on breakfast in her room, Frances spent a long time looking out of her window, brooding over the whereabouts and welfare of Don Pedro de Ravallo.

A walk was what she needed, she decided. To get out of the house – away from the talk, the questions, and the anger of her father over the loss of Bluebell.

She sighed heavily, thinking that it would have been better if Pedro had not returned the second time. There had been a tiny scar left in her heart after the first parting from the Spaniard. No doubt it would have healed fairly quickly. Now she was left with an unfulfilled longing.

She walked with firm steps matching her thoughts. She must think no more of him.

She had helped him, that was that. He had come as a member of an army dedicated to conquer England. He had had charm, courtesy and warm laughter lurking in his brown eyes. He and she had met, and had been forced to part – that was all.

But on her return to the house, her thoughts were quite different. Gone was the determination to forget him fashioned during her walk. She became restless, unable to settle to anything, ears alert for any news. She stood rigid and dry-mouthed when a messenger arrived, but it was only an invitation to attend an evening at Colston Hall, home of Sir Gerald and Lady Colston, on the following Saturday.

Normally the chance of any social function at the Hall would have been a reason for excitement and discussion, but not this time. Mrs Durville's reading of the invitation to her with a delighted smile meant nothing to Frances, and her mother was surprised when she perceived her daughter's uncharacteristic lack of interest at the invitation.

The afternoon wore on, and the strain for Frances was becoming unbearable. If only she knew that Don Pedro was safe! He should by now be a few miles away, having, she hoped fervently, made good progress during the hours of dark that had remained when he left Durville Court.

Once she went into her bedroom, locked the door carefully, and then brought out the medallion and chain that he had left with her. She held it between her hands, hoping that in some way it would enable her thoughts to reach him and know that she was praying for his safety. The medallion was the only link between her and the man now risking death in a dash across a strange country.

At about six o'clock Frances took supper with her parents and ate a little, but the food seemed to stick in her throat. She kept her eyes on her plate for most of the time for fear that her face would reveal her secret.

After supper Frances and her mother went to the latter's bedroom, to go over the clothes they were to wear on the coming Saturday at

Colston Hall. Frances knew that her mother had asked for her opinions and assistance in order to take her mind off the loss of Bluebell. This, her mother had concluded, was the cause of her daughter's depressed state of mind that day.

For some while they were busy, and when Mrs Durville had chosen a kirtle, the bodice, and the sleeves to go with it, she decided on a stand-up collar. 'They tell me, Frances,' she said, looking at her daughter, 'that the Queen herself was the first to have the fashion, but with full jewels, and that when she walked they shone like a rainbow behind her head.'

'The Queen is rich, Mother,' replied Frances, opening a box of pins, 'and she can have any fashion she chooses.'

Mrs Durville sighed. 'Yes, I suppose you are right.' Then she smiled at her daughter. 'But yet you and I, Frances, are richer than the Queen. We have your father, and the Queen is a spinster.'

Frances nodded, understandingly. 'I am thankful, Mother, but the Queen has loved, and is fortunate in that respect.'

Something in Frances's voice made her mother raise her head until they were gazing at each other through the mirror. Frances noticed the fine lines radiating from her mother's eyes down to her cheeks. Her mother must be tired. At once she felt how selfish she had been that day, thinking of no one but herself.

She placed her hand tenderly on her mother's shoulders. 'Father will fall in love with you all over again when he sets eyes on you in this dress.'

Mrs Durville's answering smile of pleasure was touched with fondness. She got up from the chair and patted her daughter's hand. 'Come now, Frances, it is your turn. You are the important one. Your life is only begun, and you have the choice of all the young men. Just when you least expect it, the right man will come along.'

Frances regarded herself in the mirror without enthusiasm. The fine clothes could not hide the sadness within her, nor give back the vitality which had been drained away during the previous hours.

She turned away, forcing a smile for her mother's sake. 'You are very good to me, Mother,' she said, kissing her on the forehead. 'But I am tired now, and...' She broke off as she heard her name being called. She glanced questioningly at her mother, then hurried to open the bedroom door.

'Frances!' It was her father's voice, and there was a strong, exultant note in it as he hurried up the stairs. 'They've caught the thieving scoundrel that took your horse. A Spaniard, would you believe!'

Frances leaned heavily against the banister. Her father's voice seemed a long way off. The stairs seemed to be moving.

'Jesiah was in the village, saw the soldiers and recognised the horse. They caught him near Ponford. They're taking him up to the Hall. You see, Frances, I said all would be...' He stopped in surprise at the look of anguish on her face.

'Oh, Father,' she murmured, and then she

crumpled to the floor before he could catch her.

When she came round she found herself looking into two anxious faces above her, their shadows thrown large upon the ceiling of her bedroom by the candelabra Captain Durville held.

She gazed up at him, his words sounding again in her ears. Her memory returned, and the fear with it. 'What will happen to the Spaniard, Father?'

Her father gave a little shrug. 'Sir Gerald will find out his rank and position, and whether the fellow is worth keeping for ransom. If not, they'll hang him or put him to the sword.'

'When?' The sound was tiny in the bedroom.

'If Sir Gerald has settled down for the night, then it will be tomorrow. If he's not too tired, the matter will be decided tonight,' replied her father.

Frances started up from the pillow, but two pairs of gentle hands eased her back again.

She must get out of the house quickly, she told herself. Reach Pedro before the soldiers got him to the Hall.

Her mother hesitated. 'You must remain the rest of the night in bed, Frances, then tomorrow we shall send for the doctor.'

'I will – I am much better.' Her mother still seemed uncertain. Frances wanted to scream at her to go. Her nerves were frayed. There was so little time. 'You and Father may go and not worry, Mother. I shall go straight to sleep without hindrance now. Rest assured.' Then, to her impatient relief, they departed with an anxious backward glance after she had turned a cheek for each of them to kiss.

No sooner was the door closed than she leapt from the bed. She had no clear idea of what she was going to do to aid the captive Spaniard, but knew that she must rescue him from the soldiers and almost certain death at the Hall.

She flung her cloak around her shoulders. It had a big hood and it would hide her face.

She moved towards the door and opened it carefully. The gallery was empty. Once outside the house she dashed across the dark courtyard as fast as her clothes would allow to the stable. This time she did not care if Casper was there – only one thing mattered now. To get between Don Pedro and his captors.

There was no time for the choice of any particular horse. Flinging herself on to the back of the closest one, she raced across the fields in the direction of the Hall.

The Hall was about a mile distant, and she knew every inch of the way, as well as the short cuts. She stopped the horse some ten yards within the forest and close to a spot where the foremost trees were wide apart, giving her a good view of the road.

Some distance to her left up the rough road was the huge outline of the Hall with its turrets and towers and lights discernible in many rooms. She dismounted and edged nearer the road and listened, but only the heavy breathing of her horse behind her disturbed the night. Was she too late? Was Pedro already being tried and sentenced?

Suddenly, with a shock that left her feeling weak, a group of horsemen appeared some hundred yards away. She mounted her horse in scrambling haste, then crouched behind its neck, as still as the tree trunks around. She could see six horsemen with helmets, a seventh without. Pedro? Her eyes fastened on him for an instant, then on the soldiers. Two in front, two either side and two bringing up the rear. The road narrowed opposite where she was hidden, with a ditch running on its other side.

Suddenly, Frances knew what she was going to do. The two leading soldiers came abreast of her, then passed, but because the road narrowed at that point, the next one on her side and flanking Pedro dropped back a yard or two. Frances felt sick. Her throat was so constricted that she felt she would not raise a whisper. She would fail miserably. For a second there was a gap in the escort's ranks.

She jerked upright from behind her

horse's neck. 'Bluebell, to me, to me. Pedro, here,' she shrieked, wheeling her mount around at the same time. Her voice rang and echoed in the surrounding forest. The sound was a mixture of fear and courage.

There was momentary confusion in the escort's ranks. Frances, looking back and ready to flee when Pedro broke through, saw Bluebell veer sharply to the left, her quarters knocking the nearest soldier and his horse stumbling into the shallow ditch on that side.

Then Bluebell and Pedro were charging across the road. For one sickening instant, she thought horse and rider were going to crash into the trees bordering the opening, but miraculously they passed between them, and she just glimpsed Pedro hurtling toward her as she shouted frantically over her shoulder for him to follow her.

Behind them the escort was in some disorder and indecision for a minute. None of the soldiers knew whether another force was awaiting them within the trees or preparing to attack them, having now freed the Spaniard.

A half mile from her home, Frances came to an abrupt halt in a hollow half-filled with mist. Bluebell was reined in quickly a few yards away.

'Make haste! Make haste, Pedro,' she gasped. 'Ride! Go now, while you are free.'

But Pedro flung himself from the horse and ran across to Frances's side and spread out his arms up to her, and her whole being filled with longing when she heard him breathlessly exclaim:

'My Francesca! How can I go without giving thanks again? When I heard your voice, I…' He reached up and grasped her hands, putting them to his face.

She leaned down from her horse, feeling that her heart was in many pieces. 'Please, Pedro, please,' she implored, 'go before it is too late. They cannot be far behind.'

His hands slid slowly and reluctantly from hers, and he turned to mount Bluebell again. Then, to her utter surprise, he turned and was dashing quickly back towards her.

'Francesca!'

There was something in his utterance of the name as it came across the darkness between them which melted her heart completely. Never would she be able to explain or understand why she slid from the horse to face him.

'I cannot go,' he said. 'I must tell you first. You are my life, Francesca. I love you.'

Her ears were filled with the murmuring of her name. For one more ecstatic fraction of time they held each other in oblivious joy. But Frances was the first to appreciate the cold, dangerous world still around them. Was that a glimmer of a lantern in the forest? She stood back from him, grasped his hand. 'My love, quickly. There is little time.' She slapped Bluebell on the flank. 'Away, Bluebell, away!' As the horse cantered away, she cried urgently: 'Come with me, Pedro. To my house. I will hide you.' He helped her up on to her horse, and then he flung himself behind her, and they were flying fast across the fields towards safety.

For Frances, that mad gallop became a ride on a cloud caressed along by a summer breeze. Joy transcended any other feeling. That this man, arms wrapped around her, sitting close behind, had spoken his love for her! She and Pedro could face the danger together, she knew it.

Near to her home they dismounted quickly and approached the stables on foot. If fortune favoured them, nobody would know that the horse had been ridden that night. There was no sound from the interior of the stables, and Frances hoped that it was too early for Casper to turn to bed. The horse was only too ready to return to quiet and more restful quarters, and with a grateful pat from its mistress, trotted into the interior of the stables.

Then, clasping each other's hand tightly, they ran, Frances leading, down the path to the beach. She would hide Pedro in the cave at the water's edge. She could not risk taking Pedro into the house. It was too early. Besides, the soldiers might want to search it.

Inside the cave they clung together, gasping, and neither spoke for a moment. Frances felt exhausted from the strain and high tension of the last hour. His arms tight about her, he spoke in his own language, then said:

'Oh, Francesca, if I die tomorrow, I have already been to heaven.'

She tautened a little at his words. 'No! Do not say that, Pedro. You must live tomorrow and tomorrow and all the tomorrows for me.' She reached up and cupped his face in her hands as she spoke.

'How I love you, Frances.'

'We are together now, beloved Pedro. We must never be parted again.'

She moulded into his passionate embrace and long kiss. Afterwards she leaned against him weakly. 'I must go,' she said anxiously. 'I must get back to my room before they discover that I am not there.'

'Always, it seems, we have to leave each other, but I must not endanger your life any further.' He relinquished his hold on her reluctantly.

'Some day, my love,' said Frances tenderly, 'we shall be together freely and in peace.'

She felt her companion shiver, and realised that he was only thinly clothed. 'Take my cloak,' she said, unfastening it and putting it around his shoulders. At first Pedro declined, but she insisted. 'I would not have you freed from the soldiers for you to risk dying of cold here.'

He caught her to him again. By the little light there was she saw him smile.

'Stay here, beloved. You will be safe for the present. Watch for the water when the tide comes in. I will come to you when I can and bring food and drink.'

Frances need not have worried; she reached her bedroom without seeing anyone. She got into bed, and fell into an exhausted sleep almost immediately.

When she awoke, it was daylight. The day was overcast and there was little movement in the trees, and the sea lay grey and flat and well below the shingle. It had been going out last night when she had taken Pedro into the cave. It would be on the turn now.

That meant that soon Pedro would have to leave the cave and seek a hiding place elsewhere. She must get out quickly to him, not only to take food, but to discuss with him where else he could be hidden when the tide came in.

Downstairs she endured a battery of anxious enquiries from the household as to her health. She blamed the fainting of the night before on a sick headache, and excused herself for the size of her breakfast, saying that now she felt better and was possessed of great hunger. This brought glad relief to the faces of her parents, happy to see that their daughter was feeling so much improved.

In reality, she wanted the food for Pedro, and most of what she made disappear from the table passed quickly into the pockets of her dress.

On the pretence of going for a walk, Frances left the house. She saw that the incoming sea was already licking at the rocks a few yards below the cave. Nearing it, she called out Pedro's name. Then, after glancing backward towards the house to make sure that no one was watching her, she slipped inside.

For a moment they stood staring at each other, as if meeting for the first time, then Pedro gave a slight bow, saying: 'Señorita Francesca. Welcome to my home by the sea.'

Their kiss was passionate, and when he released her she laid her head against his chest.

His chin rested against her hair. 'Brave Francesca, I knew you would come when you were able.'

She felt him shiver slightly. She stepped away from him suddenly, exclaiming: 'In truth Pedro, I lose my senses when I am with you. Here you are cold and hungry and I am laden down with food in my pockets for you.'

So saying, she brought out an assortment of biscuits, bread, sweet cakes, and pushed them into his hands.

Pedro smiled at her. 'And no porridge,' he said, a teasing note in his voice.

Frances smiled back in return. 'It was not

the kind of food I could carry easily to you. No doubt you are glad.'

'No, Frances, I shall remember English porridge. It helped me to live. You fed me. I was like a child. You have not forgotten?'

The look in her face gave Pedro his answer. She caressed his cheeks with her fingers. 'How could I? I think even then I began to love you.'

As soon as he had eaten an edge of water appeared in line with the bottom of the cave, making a quiet, shirring sound, and then draining away quickly through the shingle.

On seeing it, Frances exclaimed: 'See, Pedro, the sea is coming up. Soon you will have to seek shelter elsewhere until the tide goes down again.'

Her companion nodded, then remarked calmly: 'I do not fear the sea now, Francesca. I have much to thank it for. Did it not bring me to you?'

She nodded. How could she forget the fact? She stood up. 'I must go, Pedro. They will be wondering where I am. They will know that I cannot walk along the beach when the tide is in.'

Then, after giving him a quick hug, she left him after promising to see him again whenever it was possible later in the day.

Nobody looking at her that afternoon, as she bent dutifully over her needlework, could have guessed at her thoughts and the secret that she carried within her regarding Don Pedro de Ravallo and herself.

Suddenly the parlour door opened. Startled for a moment out of her wishful imaginings, Frances glanced up. It was her mother. From her manner it was obvious she had something to tell, and was impatient to tell it. Mrs Durville began to talk rather breathlessly, as soon as she had closed the door.

'It is strange, Frances, but I never know where to find you these days.' Frances had no time to reply to this before her mother imparted in glad and excited tones: 'I bring good news. Bluebell is back!'

She feigned surprise at her mother's announcement. She had expected the horse to return sooner or later, but her pleasure at hearing of it was genuine. Vagabonds, soldiers, anyone could have stolen it.

'Yes,' said her mother, moving over to the window, 'some soldiers have returned her. Look.'

Frances peered through the window at Bluebell and four soldiers on horseback, and the figures of her father and John talking up at them. Alarm filled her. Suppose they wanted to search the house and its surrounds?

Then, to her immense relief, the soldiers turned their horses and began to move across the courtyard and down the drive, and John and her father, talking earnestly together, went out of view as they made their way towards the front door.

Mrs Durville fetched her work basket and placed it in determined fashion on the parlour table. 'My mind is made up. I have been thinking, Frances, about that bodice. I am going to alter...'

What her mother was going to alter she

never knew, because just then her father entered the room, brushing the rain from his clothes as he did so. He began to warm his hands at the fire, spreading the palms out towards it. Then, having warmed them to his satisfaction, he turned to his wife and daughter.

'The ruffian escaped last night as the soldiers were taking him to the Hall,' he said.

Frances affected surprise, but her mother's was real. 'The Spaniard?' she gasped.

Her husband nodded, frowning.

'And he is yet free?'

'Yes. They found the horse this side of the village.'

Frances kept her head bent, but her hands had ceased to occupy themselves.

There was a note of alarm in her mother's voice when she spoke again. 'But Richard, are we not in danger?'

He shook his head, frowning. 'No, I'll wager the Don and his friends are well away from here now, but I cannot understand why they left the horse.' He shrugged. 'Perhaps they thought it would be recognised in the daylight.'

'There are others, Richard?' asked Mrs Durville, a hand to her breast.

Her husband nodded at the window, in the direction of the departed soldiers. 'They say there were several hidden in the trees at the side of the road. After a skirmish, they retreated, and our men followed for some distance into the woods, but one of the soldiers fell and the man was injured, so they did not proceed after the Spaniards further.'

Frances, who had stiffened suddenly when her father had mentioned that others were involved, now relaxed in relief and smiled inwardly at the thought of the face-saving excuse by the soldiers. Having failed to guard the prisoner, they had lied. What would they have said if they had known that only one very frightened young woman had been hiding on the edge of the woods?

Captain Durville strode over to the window and looked out, frowning heavily in puzzled fashion. After a short time he spoke again. 'One thing my mind cannot understand in this affair.'

Two pairs of feminine eyes swung in his direction.

'And what is that, Richard?' said his wife.

He turned away from the window into the room again. 'The sergeant at arms swears that the voice he heard from the wood shouting commands at the Spaniard was English!'

Mrs Durville also looked puzzled at this, while Frances suddenly found work for her fingers again, and her heart began to beat quickly.

Captain Durville shook his head in bewilderment. 'I think the man is mistaken, I cannot believe him, though I did not doubt his word to his face.' He sat down at the table. 'Why,' he said, staring ahead, 'should Spaniards rescuing a comrade speak in English?'

'Because, Richard,' said his wife with irrefutable logic, laying pins and scissors on the table, 'they must be English.'

Frances's heart sank at her mother's words, while her father still stared at his wife with a look that became sharper every second. The obvious had, it seemed, escaped him until now.

He said, fiercely: 'Then who are these traitorous dogs who would free an enemy?' He banged the table with his fist, and his glance swept from his wife to his daughter.

Frances shrank inside herself and bent even more closely over her needlework. She could feel his eyes upon her. To her relief, her mother, unknowingly, came to the rescue.

'But, Richard, was not the Spaniard brought through the village?' Captain Durville's eyes switched to his wife as she went on: 'So if there were any sympathisers with the Spanish cause present, they would have seen the prisoner and horse, and our horses are well known to many.'

Her husband relaxed and leaned back in his chair, seemingly reassured. Then he said in quiet tones: 'I shall be shamed to my dying day if anyone of my household were found to have turned traitor.'

'Oh, Richard!' exclaimed his wife. 'The

people who serve us and work here are most loyal, and would be hurt to hear you speak so.'

Captain Durville's face lost its stern look, and he gave a small sigh and looked affectionately at both women. 'I am only thinking of the safe keeping of those dear to me.'

Frances summoned up her courage, looked up and spoke, her voice sounding strange after her long silence. 'Why all this fuss, Father, over one poor Spaniard? Can one man be so important?'

'Yes, Frances, he can,' replied her father firmly. 'Does not the plant grow from a seed?' He smiled then and held out his hand to his wife. 'Come, Marion. I have some new material to show you. Already we are trading again, despite the Spaniards. I had forgotten about it, and now you must see it.'

Mrs Durville uttered a cry of delighted surprise, rose and took her husband's arm. 'Will you come, too, Frances?'

'No, Mother, thank you,' she replied, glad to be over what had been a very trying half hour. Besides, she had other plans. 'I think I will go and look at Bluebell and make her acquaintance again,' she lied.

'Dress warmly, for the day is poor,' said her mother, and preceded her husband through the door.

'It is a new kind of cloth – I think you will like it, Marion. It is a heavy…'

Her father's voice faded as the door closed, and Frances was left alone to ponder the fact that no pardon could be expected from her father for Don Pedro de Ravallo if he was caught.

Chapter Four

Anyone knowing Frances and seeing her making her way ostensibly to the stables some short while after the conversation with her parents, would have been surprised at the large figure she had suddenly acquired.

They would have been even more surprised to know what it was that gave the look of unaccustomed stoutness to the daughter of Captain and Mrs Durville.

Underneath a long cloak she had hidden towels, dry clothes, a hat, and anything she could obtain to make Pedro's life a little less damp and more comfortable.

But she carried something else in her cloak pocket, the chain and medallion that he had given to her. Now she was going to return it.

Hastening down the path, she saw that the tide had receded again and was now beyond the lower wall of the cave entrance. As she passed the trees she called his name softly but there was no answer, and she guessed that he had gone back into the shelter of the cave.

She found him wet and cold, but cheerful all the same, and the happiness in his eyes when she appeared was worth all the risks and danger she had endured since his coming.

'How long it seems since I saw you, Frances,' he said. 'The world has slowed since you left me.' They embraced, and she forgot the rain, the sea, the soldiers. Everything vanished except the cave. She and Pedro were alone in the world.

Then Frances realised how wet his clothes were, and she was appalled. 'These clothes – you must take them off, Pedro. Otherwise you will become ill.' She grabbed a towel and began to dry his hair, looking anxiously into his face.

He stopped her. 'There is no need, Francesca. As long as you love me, no harm will befall me.' But despite his protestations, he shivered visibly, and she insisted that he put on the dry clothes she had brought at once.

With her back to him she gazed out at the still falling rain.

After a few minutes she heard him say: 'There, now I am fit to receive the English lady.'

She turned and fell into his waiting arms. He looked tenderly down at her face, tracing the outline of it with his fingers. She felt the tension go from herself. After the last hour, it was good to relax in Pedro's embrace, even if it was to be only for a short while.

She sighed at the thought which occurred to her suddenly, brought on from something her father had said earlier.

'You sigh, my Frances,' he said softly, stroking her hair. 'I know that I have caused you great worry, and I am sorry.'

'No, Pedro, it is my own thoughts that plague me a little.'

'Tell me of them.'

She raised a serious face to his. 'If,' she said slowly, 'if you were free to return to Spain, Pedro, would you still fight against England?'

For a moment his face clouded to match the gloom of the day outside, and he glanced away from her. It was as if her question had reminded him of the original mission that had brought him to England's shores. But when he answered it was in a light, bantering tone. 'How could I turn against the country that has raised the Señorita Francesca?' Her gaze remained anxious, and Pedro spoke again, but this time his tone was deeply serious. 'I am finished with war – I want no part of it.' Then a look of deep, burning love came into his dark eyes, the look that she was beginning to know well, as he added: 'There can be no escape for me, Frances. I am a prisoner of the heart – your prisoner.'

They clung together, Frances full of joyous love at his words; but then she withdrew from his arms reluctantly. She must not be too long away from the house, and she must give him the latest news before leaving him.

'I must tell you, Pedro, that the soldiers came to the house earlier this afternoon. They have brought my horse back with them. It was found near the village. My father spoke with the soldiers. They think that you and some others are on the way to one of the ports.'

Upon seeing his puzzled look, Frances went on to explain to him all that the soldiers had told her father. They laughed quietly together when she related to him how the soldiers had said that there had been a band of men hidden in the woods to aid his dash for freedom.

She glanced outside the cave and saw that the rain had ceased. She knew that she must return to the house quickly; it was dangerous to stay any longer.

Then she remembered the medallion and chain in her pocket. Pedro watched her as she brought it out and placed it in his hand.

'It is yours, Pedro,' she said, smiling. 'Do you remember? You gave it to me the night you galloped away on Bluebell.' She paused and sighed. 'I thought never to see you again. Even then my heart was yours.'

He looked down at the object in his hand. 'And mine was yours,' he replied. 'As I rode away, I was in black despair. What was my freedom worth without you, Francesca?'

She gripped his hand in a reassuring gesture. 'We are together now, Pedro. I pray that we might be together always.'

He made to give her the medallion back,

saying: 'Take it, Francesca. It is yours.'

She shook her head. 'No, Pedro, give it to me when we are free to walk together. Besides, someone may see it, and that could mean danger for you.'

Her companion nodded understandingly, and held the chain spread out between his hands. Then he said: 'When you have been away from me, all my thoughts have been on us, Francesca.' A slightly troubled look appeared on his face as he continued: 'But I have no house, no position, and no money. I own nothing. What do I have to give you?'

'It does not matter. You have given me love. I ask for nothing more,' she said quickly and sincerely.

'Then, shall we tie our hearts together with this chain, Francesca? I have no ring to give you.'

Her eyes had given her answer long before her softly uttered words: 'I will wear it for ever.'

Whereupon he removed the medallion, took her hand and began to wind the chain around her finger. 'I would have waited until I was free to ask for your hand in marriage, my Francesca,' he said, 'but if heaven is unkind to me, and I am caught, it will be too late.'

'No, no! That must not happen again,' she exclaimed.

Pedro finished winding the length of chain round her finger. Fear for him showed on Frances's face at his words. He hastened to allay her fear. 'Perhaps,' he said hopefully, 'it will not be long before Felipe and your Queen have drawn up a plan for peace.'

'But what if there is no peace between our countries, dear Pedro?' she asked, gazing up at him as if her life depended on his answer.

A gleam of humour appeared in the Spaniard's erstwhile serious eyes, and he smiled. With a flourish of his arms and a little bow he said: 'Then I will ride to London and ask your Queen for the hand of the most beautiful lady in England!'

She touched him tenderly on the cheek in acknowledgement of his attempt to cheer her. 'I hope you never have to,' she said with a small, sad smile. 'I pray that our two countries will soon be at peace.'

He gathered her to him, saying confidently: 'When next you come to me, we shall arrange our wedding day.' Then he added: 'Though you will think my manners as rough as this cave to talk about that in such surroundings. Some day,' he went on, 'we shall not hide away. I will show the world your beauty, and nothing else will ever frighten or worry you.'

Frances stared into her companion's face before saying softly: 'Wherever you were, Pedro, that would be my home, even this cave. All I wish is that we be together always.' She paused, and in the gathering dusk lost herself in his eyes. 'I do love you, Pedro,' she whispered.

Their gentle, tender kiss became a passionate, breathless clinging to each other, as if it were to be the last time they would see each other.

The cold, damp, gloomy cave became for a short while rosy-hued. A special sun burst through and encased them in its warmth, and in the cave where she had played as a child, Frances found ecstatic joy as a woman. And the ever-present danger surrounding them both was forgotten.

But the world had changed once again by the time she left the cave and hurried up the shingle towards the path. It was dark, and she had stayed out longer than she had intended to, but in her happy state of mind the path became a smooth, effortless ascent illuminated by stars beneath her feet, and the dripping trees, bowed their approval on either side.

The figure standing at the top of the path caused her to cry out with shock. 'Father!' She had not seen him until the last moment.

'You have been gone this last hour. You were not in the stables,' he said, and there was relief in his voice at seeing her.

She was glad of the darkness to hide her expression. She thought quickly. 'I looked in at Bluebell, then a headache came over me. The sea air cleared it.'

They began to walk back to the house. 'Casper said he had not seen you; I began to fear,' said her father, adding: 'I am wary with those Spaniards about.' He put his arm around his daughter's shoulder affectionately, but on feeling the wetness of her cloak he exclaimed: 'Your cloak, Frances, it is soaking. Where have you been, my child?'

The cloak! It was the one Pedro had worn when sheltering earlier under the trees. She had left him her dry one, and was bringing the wet one back.

'I – I sheltered under the trees – it was raining so hard. I shall be all right, Father,' she said hastily.

Captain Durville removed his own short cloak. 'Give yours to me, Frances, or in truth you will take cold.' He placed his across her shoulders.

Dear Father, thought Frances. To him she was still a young girl – never a woman. A child to be protected and watched over. How sad that she could not confide in him now, when at last she had fallen in love. The most important thing in her life had come to pass, and she had to remain silent.

They were approaching the back door. She became aware that her father was speaking to her.

'You do not hear me, Frances?'

'Sorry, Father.'

'Your thoughts were away from me. Is it the pain in your head?'

She took the excuse offered. She nodded. 'A little, Father. It is nothing – it will pass.'

Captain Durville hurried his daughter into the passage, and then into the hall with its great fire burning. Then he drew his chair up directly in front of it, and guided her down gently into it.

He leaned down over her and said in kindly fashion: 'It seems that you have become a lonely child since my return – taken to going off on your own these days. I can never get you to myself.' He patted her shoulder and said sternly, his eyes twinkling in the firelight and belying the tone: 'Mistress Frances, as Captain of this ship I order you to remain in this chair until I return with something to warm your vitals and drive the cold out.'

She reached up and tugged at his beard gently and fondly. 'You are the most handsome father a girl ever had.'

Captain Durville went off towards the kitchen smiling with pleasure, and thinking with pride that he had a very special and beautiful daughter. Far from looking ill, she had looked radiant and happy in the firelight, whether she had been in the rain or not!

As for Frances, she was content just to face the fire and bask in its warmth. Suddenly she was tired, and two emotions were present in her mind. One was happiness in her love for Pedro and his for her. The other was of receding fear – a fear that had been kindled on seeing her father at the head of the path earlier. A few more minutes, and he would almost certainly have caught Don Pedro de Ravallo and herself together in the cave.

Later that night, she sat at her window and waited for Pedro to appear beneath it as soon as he saw the candlelight go out in the bedrooms, and the household settled to sleep in the darkness.

She had arranged that she would drop food, which she had smuggled into her bedroom, to him as he stood below. The night was dark and fine, but the sea breeze held a foretaste of the winter winds to come.

Frances shivered and snuggled into her gown. Poor Pedro, how cold he must be out there. The tide was coming in, and he would be making his bed under the trees.

She gave thanks that it was not quite winter yet. If it had been, she doubted whether he could have survived. Even if he had, the leafless branches of the winter trees would not have provided a hiding place during the time the sea filled the cave.

Suddenly her tired eyes caught a movement below, and soon she could see Pedro's face looking up. Her heart leapt at his coming, and she quickly took hold of the pillowcase which she had made ready, containing the food and wine. Then, leaning downwards from the window, she dropped it, praying that it would fall directly into his eager hands. It did, the package halting above the ground near the face, with barely a sound to tell of its safe arrival. Frances blew him a kiss, and wished she could follow it. Then she watched his shadowy figure merge into the night.

She closed the window slowly, reluctantly, as if the act would take him from her sight for ever, the man who had by now become the centre of her world.

Sleep did not come easily to Frances as she lay in her bed that night, nor did she want it to, not until she had found a solution to her problem of where to hide Pedro next. She was quite certain that he could not continue to alternate between hiding in the cave and beneath the trees. It was now autumn, with the prospect of colder weather to come, and she was anxious that his health should not suffer from exposure to the constant damp of the cave and the drenchings he sometimes received outside.

Besides that consideration was the fact

that her father would become curious if she were seen coming from the small beach too often, and particularly when the weather was poor. As well as that, she had heard her father saying to John Standard that they must continue to keep a sharp lookout in the vicinity of the house, just in case any more Spaniards were about.

One other aspect of Pedro's plight troubled Frances. She had begun to notice a hint of impatience in him at his confinement to the small area of the cave and beach. She realised that it was only natural, now that he was feeling stronger, that he wanted to do something positive to try to bring about a solution to their problem. They both wished to live more normal lives, and not be in fear whenever they met, but she dreaded the thought that one day he would lose caution and be caught.

The unpleasant fact was that, as long as Spain and England were in a state of war, Pedro would have to remain her hidden love. For either to declare their feelings in public would cost them their lives.

Frances turned in her bed as if the action would shake her brain into some form of sharp activity and produce a solution. Outside her window the stars twinkled in a moonless sky, and one star in particular, which had a bluish shine to it, caught and held her gaze, leaving her thoughts free for more practical things.

Should she hide Pedro in the old schoolroom again? She shook her head in answer to her own question. That had sufficed when he had only been expected to stay the night, or a few days at the most. It would be too dangerous over a long period. She sighed in desperation, and the blue star continued to hold her unseeing gaze.

Some other place. The words repeated themselves in her mind over and over again. Then almost without realising it, her lips formed the words: some other person. Her consciousness fastened on to the alteration. Why not? Somebody else to hide Pedro in a new place. But who? Whom could she trust?

Frances concentrated her thoughts on the members of the household. Her father? The thought of him in relation to Pedro made her smile grimly. The idea of help from her father she dismissed quickly. He was the one person she could have trusted above anyone – except on this one particular question.

What of her mother? She felt that she could count on some help from that quarter. Mrs Durville would have some sympathy for another woman caught in a dilemma of love, even if the man involved was a Spaniard. But Frances frowned doubtfully in the quiet of her room. Her mother was too close to her father. They loved each other very much, even after many years of marriage, and it was impossible to believe that her mother could keep the secret of her daughter's love for the Spaniard from her husband for very long. Not intentionally would her mother give the secret away, but something would be bound to draw Captain Durville's attention to his wife's behaviour. It was a risk that could not be taken, when Don Pedro de Ravallo's life was at stake.

But who else was there? Alice? Frances dismissed that person as the keeper of a secret immediately her name came to mind. Good points she had, and a worthy woman she certainly was, but so highly strung that the truth would surely burst out of her one day before she realised it. The information would be too great for her to carry alone.

Flora? Frances's thoughts slowed down and lingered on the much-loved cook. Practical Flora, grey-eyed and warm-faced. Many were the secrets – small ones, it was true – that she had concealed during Frances's childhood. Never once had a childish confidence been betrayed. Would Flora keep a most serious and dangerous adult one, though?

Frances turned her mind to the other members of the Durville Court household. The maids Elspeth and Mary: too young, giggly, and the contemplation of the frightful penalty if caught would be too much for them. Nothing would be gained by allowing them to know anything of the affair, Frances decided.

That left Casper and Jesiah. The same applied to Casper as to the maids. Youth and frequent visits to the village, and maybe a touch of bravado inside his circle of friends, and the secret would be out. The stable would have served as a new and dry hiding place for Pedro, but it was also too easy a place to be searched by anyone.

And Jesiah? At Durville Court for the last five years, a quiet man, not easily known, but conscientious in the performance of his duties at the house. His loyalties would not permit him to hold his tongue.

Again, Frances crossed a name from her mental list.

Her thoughts side-stepped the obstacle of John Standard, and fastened on his wife again. She knew that if Flora would agree, Pedro could use the small room near the rafters above the bedroom in her cottage.

If only, thought Frances, it would be possible. He would be safe and well, and she herself would have peace of mind. Their joy and their love for each other were spoilt by the constant strain and tension that each day brought while Pedro had to bide his time in the cave and in the open. Her spirits began to rise hopefully, but then fell just as quickly when the figure of John, whom she had deliberately avoided thinking about, came into her mind.

He was a kind and protective man, jealous of the position given to him by her father at the house. A very familiar figure, grown older in the service of the Durville family, and like her father, an Englishman to the last. He had spent many years of his life in campaigns against the Spaniards before being put ashore, and a man like that, Frances reasoned, was not likely to take kindly to having a Spaniard living under the same roof, and one who had been until recently a member of the army sent to conquer England.

Perhaps Flora could persuade her husband to help hide Pedro but Frances did not hold much hope of that happening. Besides,

Flora herself had yet to be approached, and she might easily be too frightened, so that the plan would come to nothing before it ever reached John's ears.

Tiredness at last began to make Frances's gaze slide away from the blue star, and her eyes closed. Tomorrow she would ask Flora, she decided, but in the meantime hope that she could somehow influence John Standard to deal kindly with an erstwhile enemy.

The next morning found her standing in the doorway of the kitchen and waiting, somewhat apprehensively, for Flora to straighten from her concentrated stirring of the pot over the fire. Now that the moment had come, Frances did not know how to begin but she was glad to see that Flora was alone in the kitchen, though Alice and the other maids were somewhere about and could appear at any time.

Flora looked up to see Frances, and gave a little start of surprise at finding her standing there. She put a hand to her ample upper body.

'Oh, Mistress Frances! I heard nothing of you, and for a moment I thought you were a ghost.'

Frances realised that she still had her cloak and hood on from her visit to Pedro. The coming conversation with Flora had preoccupied her thoughts, and she had made straight for the kitchen on returning home without stopping to take her outer garments off. She pushed her hood from her head, gave her cloak a shake, and the raindrops spotted the kitchen floor. Winter was arriving before autumn had finished.

'I did not mean to frighten you, Flora,' she said, with a small smile of apology.

The cook shook her head. 'It's all this talk of Spaniards that's been about, Mistress Frances.' She grasped her apron bottom and patted her face. If she had not, no doubt she would have wondered at the look which came and went swiftly on Frances's face.

Flora wiped her hands, gazing expectantly at her visitor the while, and wondered what was so important that brought the Captain's daughter into the kitchen so early. How bonny had the young Frances grown, she thought, from the rosy-cheeked child whose outstretched hands had barely reached the table-top in their frequent appeals for whatever sweetmeats had been on view.

Now she noticed that those hands were held tightly, and the eyes were troubled. Also she noticed that the cheeks were paler than usual, and the open cloak over the maroon kirtle and white bodice hung a little more loosely over the comely figure than had recently been the case.

Frances glanced behind her, then said anxiously: 'Will you take a rest from your labours, Flora? I would talk with you away from here.' Flora looked surprised, but was more so when Frances further asked: 'Is John away from the cottage? I would talk with you alone. It is most important, Flora.'

The agitated manner in which she spoke left Flora in no doubt that Mistress Frances had a trouble, and was in need of help. This was not the creature of a month ago.

Something was seriously wrong.

'As always, Mistress Frances, you're welcome in our home. I have seen nothing of John this last hour. He did say he was going to help Jesiah store logs for the winter ahead.'

Relief showed on Frances's face at her words.

Flora glanced around the kitchen. 'I'd better not be too long. What your father will say if the dinner is not on the table at twelve, I dare not think about. You know the Captain – a strict man for the meal on the hour.'

A small smile brightened Frances's worried face for a moment. 'I shall answer to my father if you are late, Flora, have no worry on that account.' And as she followed the cook from the kitchen, she wished for a moment that all she had to concern herself about was the time of the meal being placed upon the family's table.

A few minutes later, they were seated together in the cottage, in a small, sombre, enclosing room – well-fitted, thought Frances, for the telling of secrets. The banked-up fire gently warmed her back as she sat, elbows upon the table, at a loss how to begin.

Opposite, out of range of the hearth, sat Flora, grey-eyed and concerned, her roly-poly arms cushioning her bosom as she leaned forward expectantly, wondering what on earth it could be that could not be said in front of her husband.

Frances looked steadily at the older woman and in great seriousness said: 'Flora, I need your help. I cannot turn to anyone else.'

Flora looked almost frightened, but then she smiled comfortably and said: 'We've solved many problems between us, Mistress Frances, in my time here. Whatever it is, I will help, you know that.'

Thus encouraged, Frances said quietly: 'I'm in love, Flora. I have given my heart.'

'Ah, Mistress Frances,' exclaimed Flora in glad tones, her face suddenly alight at the news. 'I am...' Then she stopped short. The haunted look in the eyes of the young woman opposite her was not the look of a person ready for congratulations. Suddenly she thought she understood.

'And this loose-footed rascal does not share your feelings, Mistress Frances? Is that it?' she said gently.

Frances shook her head, looking at the table. 'No, Flora, that would be a simple matter compared to the web I find myself in.'

The older woman looked nonplussed but continued to gaze at the bent head before her.

Frances raised her head to look into Flora's face for a few seconds. 'This man loves me, Flora,' she said, and then her gaze slid away to her hands. Such was the look of sadness in her eyes that Flora instinctively reached out and placed a rough hand on hers comfortingly. 'The trouble is,' Frances went on, 'he is a Spaniard.'

'A Spaniard!' Flora's face became all eyes in shocked surprise.

Words tumbled from Frances. 'I found him one night, almost dead, on the path. From the Armada. He would have died, Flora. I hid him.'

Flora rocked back on her stool and rolled her eyes to the ceiling. 'Mistress Frances, oh Mistress Frances,' she exclaimed in a hushed voice. 'Oh mercy, mercy me.' She made a characteristic gesture, raising her apron and covering her face, and muttering behind it. Then, recovering herself a little, she stared wide-eyed over the top of her apron at Frances to find the young girl shaking with a sobbing which she could not control.

All the strains and tensions of the last weeks, the fears and passions, had taken their toll of Frances, and now she could restrain herself no longer, but gave way, and her words poured from a tormented soul. 'Oh, Flora, I have a love, but yet no love. We cannot walk together. If he is found he will die. What am I to do? Rather than live like this, I will die with him.'

Flora, upset at the sight of Frances so distressed, forgot her own feelings and moved quickly to the girl's side and put a comforting arm around her shoulders. 'Oh, Mistress Frances; what a state you've got your poor self into. It's a pity to see you like this.'

'He is a good man, Flora,' said Frances tearfully, as she rested against her. 'He would wed me, but how can he? Our countries are still at war. I cannot ask my father for help. You were the only person I could turn to.' She looked up into Flora's face. 'Will you help me hide him somewhere in here, where he will be safe and well?' she pleaded, then added miserably: 'I fear for his life if he has to hide outside any longer.'

Flora was silent for a while, and Frances's head lay heavily against her breast as if all strength had drained away. Flora shook her head slowly, then exclaimed in disbelieving tones: 'A Spaniard!'

Frances nodded without speaking.

Flora heaved a sigh. 'Where is he hiding?'

'In the cave near the beach when the tide is out,' replied Frances, sitting upright again. Then, recovering herself somewhat, she told her in weary tones everything that had taken place since the Spaniard's arrival.

The apron came and went to Flora's face

several times during the telling of the story, but when it was finished, she nodded, understandingly and said: 'My mind has been troubled over you, Mistress Frances, these past weeks. Something was wrong, I was certain. I told John so. "She has a weight on her shoulders. It is not the Frances that we know." I saw it in your face. I worried, Mistress Frances, and I was going to ask but John said to keep my place and not interfere, though he himself has acquired a number of grey hairs over you.' She looked at Frances affectionately. 'Lucky the man I said who won you, Mistress Frances. But never in my life did I expect him to be a Spaniard.' With a shrug of her shoulders she added: 'But we have no sway over the matter in the heart's affairs.'

'You will like him, Flora, I know you will,' said Frances, brightening a little in relief that Flora had not yet refused to help her. She went on: 'He has a pleasant nature, and he will do you no harm, I swear.'

'Has he a name, this Spaniard of yours,

Mistress Frances?'

'Pedro – Don Pedro de Ravallo.'

'He sounds like a man of noble birth.'

'I do not care,' said Frances, and then she carried on with great feeling: 'Oh, Flora, he is the only man to have brought love for me. I knew without thinking of it.' Her look grew desperate. 'I must save him, Flora, I must!'

Flora looked worried and was silent for a moment. Outside the heavy rain streamed from the roof and spattered noisily on the ground by the door. She broke the silence by sighing, then said: ''Tis a great trouble indeed you have brought with you this day, Mistress Frances. And,' she continued, 'it is full of danger, this thing you would have me do.'

'Yes, it is true,' replied Frances, looking downcast, 'but should Pedro be caught, you will not be blamed, Flora. I shall say that it was my fault – that I found him and...' Here her expression held more spirit. 'I would do this for the man that I love.'

Flora stared aghast at her for a moment.

'No! Mistress Frances, never must you do that. It would be certain – oh, I cannot bear to think of it.' She twisted the apron in her hand. 'And your poor mother and the Captain.'

Frances hastened to allay her fears. 'Have no fear on that account, it will not happen, Flora. Peace may be declared in the next few days and then the Queen will grant a pardon to Pedro.' She tried to sound hopeful, but in her innermost heart she knew that it could be years before a state of war was ended. The fact that the Armada had been defeated might not deter Philip from carrying on the war. A pleasanter thought came to her. 'When peace comes, Flora, then I shall be able to tell my father and Pedro will ask him for my hand in marriage.' To Frances it all sounded so simple, merely by saying the words.

But Flora looked doubtful when she spoke. 'It frightens me to my death at what your father would do if he knew there was a Spaniard so near to the house.' She shook her head at the thought.

Frances did not dwell on the awful consequences – they had been in her mind far too many times.

For a minute the younger woman and the older, seated side-by-side, were preoccupied with their thoughts. Then Flora said:

'But where can we hide him here, Mistress Frances? There is but this room and the one above.'

Frances's spirits rose a little. Her proposal had not been rejected out of hand. She shook her head. 'Have you forgotten that tiny room just below the roof?'

Flora nodded slowly in frowning consideration of the information given, but then her ample form seemed to subside to two-thirds its size as she sighed heavily at a thought. 'And have you forgotten my John, Mistress Frances?'

'Oh, no, I have not. If only you could persuade him to help me, Flora,' beseeched Frances.

Flora stared ahead at the wall opposite.

‘He thinks the world of you, Mistress Frances,’ she said, ‘as his own child, so to speak. He’d do anything rather than allow you to be hurt. But what you ask...’ She chewed her lip and murmured: ‘I just don’t know what he’ll say.’

‘Then you will speak with John for me?’ asked Frances anxiously, her eyes clinging to her older companion. ‘This man means everything to me.’

Flora gave a smile. ‘You tell the truth, Mistress Frances – it stands on your face for all to see.’ She paused, eyeing the young woman in kindly fashion. Then she said: ‘Can this Spaniard be trusted? There are rogues from all nations.’

‘Oh, yes, Flora, he can,’ affirmed Frances earnestly. ‘Did I not tell you that when he could have escaped that night, he chose instead to return here and hide and put himself in peril because of his feelings for me?’

Recollection came to Flora’s eyes. ‘So you did, Mistress Frances,’ she answered thoughtfully.

'He is not a rough man, Flora,' said Frances, the sudden lovelight shining in her eyes to the accompaniment of her words.

Flora's face became extremely serious. 'I will speak with John for you, Mistress Frances. Gladly I would help, but I hold no great promise of swaying John. He is a loyal man and loyal to your father. He will do nothing which might bring danger to him or this house, and,' she added significantly, 'he got his bad arm against the Spaniards!'

Frances knew that what Flora had just said was true. She could not have expected her to say otherwise. But would one cold and weary young Spaniard be such a threat to her father and his household that John would refuse to help when asked? How tiring and fraught with difficulty everything was, she thought.

Flora saw the hopeful look recede from the young face, and she felt sorry and hastened to raise her spirits. 'Do not worry so, Mistress Frances,' she said cheerfully. 'In my time in the service of the Captain and your mother, you've brought me a few problems to unravel.' She paused to smile, then posed the question: 'Did I ever fail?'

Frances gave a small, fond smile in return and a little shake of her head. She felt almost a young girl again bringing some trifling problem to her old friend. How she wished that her present difficulty could be solved as easily as those of her childhood had been.

'Nor shall I start now,' said Flora firmly, 'though for your sake, Mistress Frances, I hope that the peace cometh soon.'

In her heart Frances echoed those last words. Peace must come quickly, or else…

The cook rose from the table. 'Now, Mistress Frances, you will take no offence, but if I'm not to be looking for other employ elsewhere, I'd best get back to my position.'

Frances stood up and, taking hold of Flora's shoulders, planted a hard-pressed kiss on the older woman's cheek. 'Thank you, Flora,' she said gratefully. Then, with an expression of utter sincerity, she looked into her companion's face. 'Pedro is my true love, Flora, never will there be anyone else.'

The older woman gazed back at the young one facing her. She had known love herself, and recognised it when she saw it. 'I shall talk with John, Mistress Frances,' she said simply.

Chapter Five

The next few hours for Frances were plagued with misgivings about revealing her secret to Flora. Had she been foolish in doing so? Was John even now acquainting her father with the news? Would his loyalty to her father override his feeling of mercy towards a fellow human being? She comforted herself with the fact that Flora had agreed to help, and Frances was certain that she would be true to her word. But if John refused, could Flora influence him to remain silent?

Frances began to feel the strain of waiting to hear from her, and kept away from places where she was likely to meet John. By late afternoon she could not stay in the house any longer. She must get away from its confines, even for a few minutes. Her feet flew down the path to the cave. There she told Pedro what she had done.

He shared her anxiety, and said that rather than have Frances put herself any more in danger, he would give himself up. She refused his noble offer, saying that she was confident that help would be given.

She did not stay with him long, but left after assuring him that she would come to him immediately she heard from Flora. But as she raced up the path back to the house again, she was far from confident about the outcome, and her impression of Pedro's health as she left him was of a slow deterioration. It was becoming imperative that he be kept inside where regular food and warmth could be given to him.

Six o'clock came, the hour for supper. Frances ate hers nervously alone with her parents. Every moment she expected her father to get to his feet and point an accusing hand at her and denounce her as a traitor.

But nothing of the sort happened, and she began to feel that her fears of John telling all to her father were groundless. In fact, her father appeared to be in a cheerful state of mind and looking forward, so he told her and her mother, to going down to Plymouth the next day to supervise the refitting of his ships, the change back from warships to merchantmen again. He would be away about three days.

Frances was relieved to hear this piece of news. With her father gone it might be easier for Pedro to be moved to his new hiding place – provided, of course, that Flora had been able to persuade John.

As soon as she had eaten, she made the excuse that she had a letter to write, and left the parlour to await any message that Flora may have for her. Hardly was the parlour door closed behind her than the cook's head popped out from the kitchen.

Flora gave a nervous glance at the parlour

door; then, pulling up her apron until it was like a sail in front of her, whispered from behind it: 'Tonight, Mistress Frances. After dark. Bring him. The door will be open. But take care!'

With that she dropped the apron and bustled off into the kitchen again, leaving Frances feeling weak with relief. They had not failed her! John and Flora were going to open their door to Pedro.

She made her way to her bedroom not really feeling the floor of the great hall beneath her feet. Past the fireplace with its cheerful cradle of red she went, and up the stairs which had suddenly become much shallower and easy to climb.

An hour later the lovers stood hand in hand, tense and huddled against the door of the Standards' cottage. The night was very dark and chilly but fine, and Frances was thankful for the cover it provided.

Even so, she glanced nervously about. All was still. Faint light showed in the courtyard from the downstairs windows of the main body of the house. Her eyes came back to the door. The small window next to it was heavily curtained. Nothing of the inside could be seen. John and Flora had prepared for Pedro's coming.

Frances gave a smile of encouragement to Pedro in the darkness and squeezed his hand, then knocked quietly but urgently, and pushed the door open. Ushering him inside quickly, she closed the door and turned to face the occupants of the room.

Flora stood, her apron twisted between motionless hands, her attention riveted on the figure next to Frances with an avid curiosity which was tinged with a certain nervousness. John stood warily, and suspicion showed in his eyes at his first glimpse of the Spaniard. Frances noticed John's good arm across his body, the fingers lightly touched the hilt of his sword, but if he in those first few seconds gave the impression of hostility, the surroundings belied it: their message was of welcome.

The fire blazed and crackled a fanfare of

warmth, throwing a dance of shadows around the small room, while the table was laid ready with food and drink. Two candles burning away steadily joined the firelight to illuminate the table, but could not pierce the gloom of the corner by the door where Frances and the dark figure with her stood.

For a moment there was silence. John's eyes flickered from Frances to her companion, and then back again to her.

Frances spoke, trying hard to make her voice sound normal. 'Flora, John, this is Pedro – Don Pedro de Ravallo.'

Pedro emerged slowly from the shadows, letting go of her hand as he did so, and approached Flora. She half extended her hand, which he clasped and gave a little bow over.

'Señora,' he said quietly, and then gave the woman a slight smile. This received an immediate response from Flora, who executed a brief curtsey, which surprised the watching Frances.

Then Pedro turned to John, the shadowy light serving to accentuate the haggard lines and untrimmed beard of his face. His hand came from his side toward the older man. 'Señor,' he said, 'my grateful thanks for allowing me to enter your home. I shall not forget such kindness.'

Perhaps John was taken aback by his Spanish guest addressing him in English, or maybe the years of enmity between Spaniard and Englishman was too much to bridge in a few seconds. Whatever the reason, he remained staring fixedly at Pedro. A few seconds, but it seemed a lifetime to Frances.

His wife broke the silence. 'John!' she uttered in admonishing tone at her husband's apparent lack of manners to their guest.

The sound of his wife's voice stirred John into action, his hand coming slowly away from his sword top and reaching out towards the Spaniard's hand as if at any moment his fingers would be burned at some invisible fire.

The hands met and clasped – a seeming bond between the young Spanish survivor and the older Englishman now confined to the land – then unclasped as if nothing more were needed to heal the scars of years of war.

Pedro glanced at Flora, then towards Frances, saying: 'It is not the first time I have been greeted with a sword,' and the candlelight caught the flash of amusement in his eyes. Frances was glad of the dim light to hide the rush of colour to her cheeks.

John coughed – a huge cough, the sound of which reverberated around the room. Frances felt that he was somewhat disconcerted at his meeting with Pedro and she was right. John, having spent years at sea fighting the Dons hand to hand, or from behind a cannon, had had little opportunity to meet the Spaniards face to face in peace. Now one young Spaniard stood before him, under his own roof, and as a result he was at a loss for what to say or do for the moment.

His visitor put a hand against the table, and looked at the fire like a man who has seen treasure appear before him for the taking. John saw the expression, the eagerness for warmth, and responded quickly. He waved his hand at his chair at the side of the fireplace. 'Sit there and get warm, Mr ... er, Rav...' he began, then hesitated.

Pedro came to the aid of his benefactor. 'Ravallo,' he said as he seated himself gratefully before the fire. Then he looked up at John and added: 'I would prefer Pedro.' He paused to smile, then went on: 'It is a well used name in my country.'

Both women then joined the two men near the fire, the four forming a half circle around the hearth. Frances gave a silent prayer of thanks that John had accepted Pedro into his home, although he was, she saw, regarding him closely.

Flora gave a nervous glance towards the door, then addressed Pedro in a hushed voice: 'When you have warmed yourself well and eaten, John will show you where to hide.' She turned to her husband. 'You did make it ready, John?'

He did not answer, but turned to stare into the fire.

'John!' she said sharply. 'You promised.'

'Aye,' said he gruffly, speaking at last and nodding slowly, then going on in a dubious voice: 'I know not if I am right or wrong. By the Captain's life, I wish not to deceive him in this matter.' He paused and looked fondly at Frances, then went on: 'But I could not bide to see Mistress Frances so miserable, even if it meant giving shelter to a Don to cure her condition!' Then he stared down into the seated Spaniard's face. 'One thing, and then I will speak no more of the like. If any harm should befall Mistress Frances, Mr Ravallo, through your efforts, then I will reach you and deal with you afore the soldiers get you.' John's words were uttered with a steely menace in them, and Pedro looked somewhat taken aback.

Frances placed a hand comfortingly on his shoulder. She understood the older man, but Pedro was a stranger to his ways.

'John!' exclaimed Flora, consternation in her face at her husband's words. 'Do you forget that he seeks help under our roof?'

'No, wife, but Mistress Frances here is the

Captain's daughter,' he replied.

There was a short strained silence. Then Pedro rose to his feet, his face serious in the extreme as he spoke while looking at Frances.

'It is not likely that I would harm Frances, when I have a love for her which is greater than life itself.' There was such a fond look in his eyes, and the words were said with such a simple dignity, that no one could have doubted the truth of that statement.

As for John, on hearing the deep sincerity in his guest's voice, and having himself said his piece, his manner relaxed a little. He motioned towards the table. 'Now, eat while you have the chance; the Captain may call for me before the night is out.'

Flora said: 'Stay by the fire, Don Pedro. Get the damp out of your bones. I will bring the table to you.'

And so, with Pedro on one side of the fire and John on the other, the two women plied the Spaniard with food and drink. Occasionally John would ask a question and Pedro would answer, usually to the Englishman's satisfaction, and gradually the tension that had existed between the two men began to diminish.

Pedro told John all that had happened during the battle as far as it concerned himself. John listened with great interest, and his face could not conceal his delight when his visitor said:

'The English ships, Señor John, could sail nearer the wind. It seemed to us that they could turn on a golden coin.'

His host nodded in knowledgeable agreement. 'Aye, your ships were built too tall in the water.' Here the light of remembrance came into his eyes. 'I mind the time when we raked galleons from stem to stern afore they knew we were there!'

'So you have fought against my country, Señor John?'

'Aye,' he stated, a proud gleam in his eyes.

Pedro glanced at the older man's withered left arm. 'Is that from the war between our countries?' he asked.

John frowned, and Frances knowing that he disliked having attention drawn to his disability, waited anxiously for his reply.

'A musket shot,' he said at last.

'I am sorry,' said Pedro sympathetically. 'It is the fortune of war.'

'Aye,' grunted John, shooting him a look and then gazing into the fire.

Frances, standing at Pedro's shoulder, was greatly relieved to see the two men talking together, even if John was still rather suspicious of his guest. It was only natural, she thought.

Pedro spoke again, after first looking at her: 'You are a fortunate man, Señor John. Frances has a great regard for you. She has spoken a great deal about you.'

John looked a trifle uncomfortable and stood up. 'Aye,' he said simply, looking at the floor. 'In truth, I've known her since she was a child – and a bonny one, at that.'

Frances felt her face growing hot at the compliments from both men.

Then Pedro took hold of her hand and

said: 'Since my voyage with the Armada began, I have known much sadness with the loss of my friends, and being alone in a strange country. But great happiness has also come to me through Frances.'

Flora stood beaming contentedly at the young couple, while her husband shuffled his feet and coughed.

Pedro looked into Frances's flushed face and said: 'Shall Señora and Señor be the first to know that you have promised yourself to me?'

She returned his look of love and said hopefully: 'If there is peace between our countries, it will be so.'

The Spaniard turned to his host. 'Frances is going to marry me when the war is over,' he said, restrained excitement lighting up his eyes.

Flora, who seemed to have forgotten for the time being the danger attendant at the meeting in the cottage, gave a little cry of delight and kissed Frances on the cheek. Then she stepped back, a fond look on her round face. It was obvious that she had taken Pedro to her matronly heart.

John looked doubtful.

'He will ask my father first, John,' Frances hastened to say.

'Aye, Mistress Frances, maybe, but...' He shook his head. 'Knowing your father...'

'Oh, John,' said Flora, 'he will think differently when peace comes. It cannot be long at that.' She sounded irritated at the arrow of John's doubt piercing her rosy-hued bubble of romantic feeling.

'The Captain's an Englishman top to bottom,' persisted her husband stolidly. Then he added: 'The Queen might not like it, either.'

'Huh!' exclaimed Flora. 'No doubt she's had her hand kissed by many a Spaniard in her time!' She went on: 'Besides, in all the Queen's kingdom, would she know when a Spanish gentleman married an English gentlewoman? I'll wager not.' She smoothed her apron down firmly to match the tone of her words.

At this point Pedro, who had been silent

during this exchange between Flora and her husband, said gently: 'It is enough for me just to be able to see and speak with Frances under your roof, Señora, Señor. I am fortunate and give thanks to you. When I lay on the beach I had no friends in your country.' Here he swept a hand in front of him. 'Now I have three – surely more than I deserve.' He gave a glance towards the door. 'Now I have kept you in danger long enough. I will go wherever you will hide me.'

John eyed his guest for a moment, then said: 'Aye, Mr Ravallo, I'll hide you for Mistress Frances's sake, but if you're found, I know not of you.'

The Spaniard's dark eyes were solemn as he replied: 'You have my word, Señor. It will be as you say.'

At John's words, a chill of fear ran through Frances again, bringing her back to the reality of the situation. But some day she and her love would enter the cottage together in freedom to talk with John and Flora – the door would be open, and their voices normal and not hushed.

Then, unexpectedly, and at his wife's insistence, John brought out a flask of wine from a little cupboard in the corner of the room, and to Frances's surprise he produced four silver goblets as well.

He, noticing her look, exclaimed proudly as he poured a measure of the wine into each: 'The Cap'n gave them to me, Mistress Frances, and the wine. Booty from the Spanish Main.' He then handed the goblets round, but as he handed Pedro his, the gleam in his blue eyes shone wickedly in the candlelight, and seemed to grow in intensity as he remarked: 'It's the very best Spanish wine, Mr Ravallo.'

To Pedro's credit, and Frances's relief, he took the jest in good humour, and replied in turn that, that being so, it should do him much good! Then he offered a toast for a quick peace between England and Spain. When he had finished, he looked at the three people before him, and then continued in thoughtful fashion: 'I have seen only a small part of England, but I shall remember it always.' He glanced at Frances. 'For its beauty–' his eyes moved and dwelt on the older couple – 'it's kindness and mercy.' Then he turned towards the leaping flames in the grate. 'And for the fires.'

Shortly afterwards he took leave of Frances and followed John to his new and safer hiding place.

But later on in the night, when all was quiet at Durville Court, the figure of John could have been seen removing the ladder from beneath the trap door above which his Spanish guest slept. Complete trust in a foreigner – and a Spaniard at that – would come only slowly to John Standard.

And in a quiet part of the larger house, Frances slept soundly and fully for the first time for weeks, confident that for the time being, at least, her love was safely hidden away.

The weeks went by, autumn turned into winter, and nobody in the household could have failed to notice the change in Frances which had come about in this period. Now she smiled, her fair face was rounded once more, and it would have taken a close and keen observer to see the sometimes lingering anxiety which appeared in the depths of her blue eyes.

Pedro had settled down in his new home, vastly more comfortable than his last, and confined his appearances to the darker hours when he would join the Standards downstairs to eat and talk. Sometimes Frances'd manage to be present on these occasions.

Occasionally John was engaged in tasks for her father and Flora would be busy to a late hour in her kitchen. When that happened, the two lovers could snatch an hour alone, and in between a kiss and caress, they would talk of their future and their hopes of life together some day.

One aspect of Pedro's stay with the Standards was very pleasing to Frances. That was John's gradual and real acceptance of the young Spaniard. He had now taken to addressing him by his first name, and once she joined them late one evening to find both men poring over a drawing and in close conversation on the merits of the design of certain ships. Of even more significance in John's improving relationship with Pedro was, as the latter informed her, the leaving of the ladder below the trap door at night.

After a while, the couple took to meeting down by the bay, Pedro slipping out under cover of darkness, and the two walking for half an hour along the shore. It was a delight to both, but always on these occasions a figure would be following discreetly in their wake. It was John, loyal to his employer, and mindful of his duty in respect of Frances.

Two weeks before Christmas the Durville family received an invitation to attend a Ball on Christmas Eve, to be held at Colston Hall. It was to celebrate the Christmas season, and also the victory of England over Philip's Armada. Frances had attended Christmas Balls before at the Hall and had always enjoyed herself: the different male company she met, the gaudy scene, the atmosphere and gossip not to mention the dancing, all combined to make the occasion extremely pleasant.

But this year she read the invitation somewhat less enthusiastically than usual. Part of the attraction in other years of going to the Ball had been the dream that perhaps she might meet the man who would captivate her heart, and sweep her up into a passionate love. Now that man had found her, and a thousand Balls would not reveal a man she would love as much as Don Pedro de Ravallo.

She realised, however, that she would have to attend at Colston Hall. Short of being ill, it would appear strange to her parents if she did not. She could always leave early on some excuse, at least.

On the occasions since Pedro's coming, when she had been up to the Hall, she had felt uneasy away from him, and had stayed only briefly. Katherine Colston, her childhood friend, must have thought her behaviour rather odd, reflected Frances, but after the arrival of Pedro, she had had little time or inclination to bother with people from her old life.

She looked out of her window and thought about Pedro. If only they could have gone to the Ball together. How proud she would have felt to dance with him and to see the admiring glances. She sighed – it could not be. Not at the present time. Perhaps in the New Year.

She sighed again. She was certain that Pedro was the handsomest of men. Since his stay in the cottage his face had lost its haggard, hunted look; he had trimmed his beard and hair, and now looked the young man that he was.

One other thing in Frances's eyes had helped in this transformation: a new set of clothes. Gone were the old, odd-fitting ones that she had hurriedly found for him during the early days of his captivity. In their place were new garments obtained by dint of some collaboration between John and the village carter, the latter doing the journey up to London twice a week. The carter had taken the letter of order and measurements to a man's tailor in London. When the clothes were ready he had returned with them, and John had picked them up from the village. Frances herself had paid for the clothes with money saved from the allowances her father made to her.

These changes in Pedro's appearance had the effect of producing a figure who, if it had not been for the dark features and the accent, would have passed for an English country gentleman.

Christmas Eve found Frances and her parents wending their way on horseback to Colston Hall, escorted by four of Sir Gerald's men. Snow which had fallen two days previously had laid a pure white cover over the table of earth, and the crunch of hoofs and the tinkle of harness sounded loudly in the still and starry night.

How quickly the last two weeks had gone by, Frances thought. The preparations for Christmas, decorating the house, the sewing and stitching in readiness for the Ball had made the time fly.

Her thoughts turned to Pedro as they so often did when she was away from his side. She had not had much opportunity to see him that day – both her father and mother had claimed much of her time in their preparations for the function that evening.

However, she had managed, shortly before setting off up to the Hall, to see him briefly. He had been alone in the cottage, Flora still being busy in the kitchen getting ready for the next day, and John somewhere in the main body of the house.

A burning love and stark admiration in his eyes at the sight of her made Frances wish desperately that she could stay behind with him on that Christmas Eve. They had embraced, and she had promised to try and see him again on her return, which she hoped would be soon. Pedro looked so lonely, and she had felt sad on leaving him.

Soon she was passing the place where she had aided him to escape the soldiers. Thinking of it then as she rode along made her wonder how she had had the courage to do it.

She remembered how he had proclaimed his love for her just as they were going to part for ever after the frantic dash through the woods in a bid for freedom. She pulled her hood closer around her face, the frosty air chilling her cheeks. Just behind her she could hear her parents talking to each other, and see the dark figures of the front escort ahead.

It suddenly occurred to her that she really knew nothing of Pedro's background. From Spain, yes, but which part? What town or village? Had he parents alive? Brothers? Sisters? Another love, perhaps? The last thought made Frances draw in her breath sharply. She must not think of that.

He had never spoken of his former life, had volunteered no information, and Frances had never thought of broaching the subject. Falling in love and enduring the strains and fears of the last weeks had occupied all her thought and emotions, and yet, she told herself, that was not the real reason. It was simply because, deep in her heart, she was afraid that somehow the rainbow of love and happiness between herself and Pedro would fade and disappear if she questioned too much.

So busy had she been with her thoughts that Frances saw with some surprise that they were entering the large courtyard of the Hall. Lights from the lanterns over the entrance yellowed the snow, pitted and churned with the feet of many horses. A number of guests stood wishing each other good cheer, then joined still others thronging the doorway.

The escort moved away, no doubt to enjoy a few hours' celebration in their own fashion. Frances and her parents dismounted, and after handing the horses over, began to join the merry company making their way inside the Hall. But for an instant she paused. There was a light, it seemed, coming from every window. Many were the times she had visited Colston Hall, but never had seen it as it was that night.

The great house looked warm inside, and

its roof with its towers and many tall chimneys stood white against the dark sky, with columns of smoke vanishing into the night. The building appeared to hang from the heavens on several strands of grey wool. The air coming from its interior which met Frances as she followed her parents was a warm mixture of roasts and pastries, perfume and powder, beer and wine.

Once inside they were welcomed by Sir Gerald and Lady Colston. Sir Gerald bent in greeting over Frances's hand, and the thought flashed through her mind that this was the man whose word would mean death to Pedro if he was caught. Sir Gerald was pleasant to her always, but he could be ruthless, she knew, in the pursuit of his office as Sheriff.

Then he clapped her father on the back and led him away in the direction of the great hall and its merry throng, saying: 'What a victory, Captain, eh? Smashed 'em all the way back to Spain. Come, we've much to celebrate. We'll leave the women to prance in front of the mirrors for a while. If your wife is anything like mine, you will not see her for some time yet.' They disappeared from view, Captain Durville listening politely to Sir Gerald's boisterous prattle.

Then Mrs Durville and her daughter, accompanied by their hostess, entered the great hall to join those already gathered there. The merry company assembled pressed about them, absorbing them. Fires roared away, one at each end of the huge room, and candles – some caught and fastened in lanterns, others free in great holders – fluttered and cast their lights from the walls on all present. Laughter, the clink of glasses, and smoke from the men's pipes soared into the dim heights of the raftered roof. An open gallery ran the length of one side.

Frances saw Katherine talking with a small group of people some distance away. At that moment she turned her head and noticed Frances. She waved a hand, then detached herself from the group and threaded her way towards her friend. Her face showed pleasure as she approached.

'Frances! You have come,' she exclaimed. 'I saw your father, but had little chance to speak to him to ask if you were here.' The two young women exchanged an affectionate kiss. Then Katherine went on: 'You have not been here often these last weeks. I thought the end of our friendship had come.'

Frances smiled at her. 'I must have seemed unmannerly, Katherine, my spirits seemed to desert me. Perhaps it was the weather and the war.'

Katherine nodded understandingly, and gave her a searching glance. 'Whatever the ailment, you are freed from it now, I can see.' Suddenly she laughed and waved the mask she held. 'I kept it on as long as I could, but I should have become faint had I not taken it off. The heat was too much for me.'

Frances observed that a number of men and women wore masks, these to be taken off, she knew, at midnight to reveal the wearer, though the identity was usually known long before that hour.

Her eyes came back to her friend. Tall, slim, dark-haired and groomed with clothes in the latest fashion from London, Katherine was quite bold as she gazed at the men about her.

Frances, somewhat shy and retiring, felt even more so in such a large gathering, and she began to wish she had not forgotten to bring her mask. She had intended to bring it, but had left it somewhere at home.

Katherine was dressed in a low-necked bodice and French farthingale skirt, both in scarlet satin. Her bodice was connected to the open-shaped ruff by a partlet of pink and white open lacework which showed the flesh beneath. Wide sleeves of pink slashed to reveal white undersleeves ended at the wrist with matching lace ruffs. A narrow girdle of fine silverwork encircled her waist, its ends hanging below her knees to a jade pomander case.

Her eyes gleamed mischievously as she spoke in close confidential fashion to her friend. 'I would wish, dear Frances, for you to take note of a Mr Mark Ripley, ravishingly handsome if ever I saw a man.' She looked around as if searching for a sight of him.

'But why me, if this gentleman is as you say?'

'He is not, I fear, my sort,' said Katherine, turning back to her. 'I cannot see him just now, but I will find him and introduce you. I think I could match you there. You will like him.'

'But I...' began Frances, then hesitated. How could she tell Katherine that her heart had been given to a man not present, and no other man in the building or out of it held any interest for her now?

Her companion's eyes widened in mock alarm. 'Frances! Do not tell me that that fever of yours has lost you your interest in men?'

'No,' said she, laughing, 'but scarce have I entered the house before you would have me married to this Mr Ripley you speak of.'

'Well, whether you do or not,' said Katherine, smiling in return, 'I would have you meet him.'

Frances could see that she would have no choice but to resign herself to Katherine's wishes for the moment. The evening would pass, and then she could hurry back to Durville Court to the man who had already claimed her love.

And so Frances was introduced to Mark Ripley and many other honourable young men in the course of the next hour. She chatted, joined in the gossip, partook of a small quantity of the wine which flowed so freely that Christmas Eve, and quietly did her best to appear outwardly as a young woman with no cares.

She must have played the part well because once, when she found herself near her father, he insisted on introducing her to the group of people he was with. Holding her arm and patting her hand, he addressed them with great pride.

'Was ever a man blessed with such a daughter?' he asked.

Truly Frances did look beautiful, and the admiring looks of the men present served to heighten the colour in her apple-like cheeks.

Then it was time to eat from the splendid variety of well-salted meats, delicacies, spices and confectionery, set so invitingly on the gold and silver table plates.

As Frances accompanied her parents to their seats, she overheard Sir Gerald's voice near-by in conversation.

'The Queen,' he was saying, 'is in residence at Richmond this eve – she has taken to Richmond; it is a warmer box of a house for her.' There was a pause, then Sir Gerald's voice came again, and with a feeling of dismay Frances heard him say: 'I fear she will not be allowed much peace, though. Drake's already pestering her to allow him to carry the war to Spain.' His voice droned on, leaving Frances to dwell anxiously on the implication of his words.

If the Queen agreed to Drake's request, then the war could drag on endlessly. Pedro would have to remain hidden, there would be no marriage, no hope of a proper life together. She sighed at her thoughts, staring unseeingly at the food before her. On the other hand, she told herself, the Queen may not entertain Drake's plans. She might think it better strategy to allow Philip to lick his wounds, and then perhaps peace might settle between England and Spain. Frances picked at her food disinterestedly, and prayed fervently that the Queen would not let Drake have his way. If he did, Frances and Pedro would be lost.

Chapter Six

After the feasting there was dancing in which Frances took part, getting warmer and warmer by the minute. She smiled and let the men flatter her. Once she danced with her father to the good-natured objection of the younger men present, but her thoughts were elsewhere and she would be glad when it was the hour to return home.

About this time she became aware of one particular masked face. She would be talking, glance up, and there it would be. If she turned to speak to someone it was there, framed between the heads of others present. Always at a distance, watching her. A man's head. She could not see the rest of him, hidden as it was by so many people.

She was mildly surprised. Was it another suitor – someone too shy to speak? She did not think so somehow. There was something about this man that Frances felt she ought to know, but her mind refused to supply the answer just then. In any case, she had no chance in the next few minutes to think about it, as she was swept up into the dancing again with Katherine and some others.

When that particular dance was finished, she was feeling uncomfortably hot, and after excusing herself from the company she had been with, she made her way to a seat beneath the gallery upon which the minstrels played. It was cooler there, shadowy, and would perhaps hide her from the increasing attention of the young men as the midnight hour approached. She worked her fan restlessly in front of her face. She would be glad to go now. Perhaps she would get a chance to speak to Pedro for a moment when she got home, to wish him a happy Christmas.

She glanced sideways. A couple sat a few feet away unaware of the rest of the world. They were holding hands and looking into each other's eyes and speaking the language of love. Frances sighed and leaned her chin on the top of her fan. Some day she and Pedro would be like that: without fear of being seen together in public. She closed her eyes for a moment. She was beginning to feel tired. From above her head came the sound of the musicians' feet on the floor of the gallery.

Suddenly, someone spoke her name. Was she dreaming? Her eyes jerked open and she saw the white leather shoes in front of her. Her eyes moved upwards unbelievingly, recognising the clothes. The man with the mask stood looking down at her. The dark eyes held hers from behind the mask.

'Francesca,' the voice said softly.

'Pedro!' A gasp of utter amazement was forced from her. Wide-eyed, she stared up at him as her fan slipped from her fingers.

He bent to pick it up and spoke quickly as he did so, his body hiding her expression from the other guests behind him. 'Have no fear, Francesca, no one knows.'

'But … h-how? Why?' she uttered unsteadily. She moved the fan agitatedly in front of her and glanced around fearfully, but nobody seemed to be paying any attention to her and her companion.

Pedro, who remained standing, his back to most of the now noisy company, said: 'Some people were taking the air. When they returned inside, I slipped in with them.'

Frances tried to compose herself as she looked up into the eyes behind the mask. One false step and he would be finished.

He went on: 'I could not bear to think that you were here, with all these men.' He shrugged and smiled. 'I thought perhaps one would take you away from me.'

Her mouth lifted slightly at the corners, and she shook her head as if the notion were impossible.

He continued: 'They were enjoying themselves at the house, singing and making ready for tomorrow. Flora and John were busy. I did not feel like sleep. My thoughts were of you. You are so beautiful, Francesca.'

Frances gazed at the man she loved. Her heart was thudding away at the thought of the risk he was taking. 'Oh, Pedro,' she exclaimed, 'I am so frightened for you. If you are caught...' Her voice, what there was of it, trailed off. 'Go now, I beg you, Pedro, while there is time,' she beseeched him.

At that moment the musicians began to play, and the dancing began again. On hearing the sound he grasped her hand impulsively.

'Join me in this dance, Frances, and I will go the moment it is finished.'

'Do you wish to die?' she asked incredulously.

His eyes pleaded with her. He spoke confidently. 'There is no danger. I am masked. I shall speak only to you. A few minutes. I shall treasure them all my life.'

Frances wanted to refuse, and knew that she should. It was madness to do this thing Pedro was asking. And yet, as if in a dream, she allowed him to help her rise to her feet and walk with him to where the other dancers were. It seemed to her then that the music quietened and all eyes were turned in their direction. But no voice was raised, no accusation levelled at her partner, and they entered the dance.

For Frances, though, it was a mixture of ecstatic enjoyment and a fearful alertness. Their hands touched and their glances met, and they laughed and mingled with the other dancers.

Once she saw Katherine watching Pedro inquisitively, and Frances prayed that her friend would not get near enough to speak to him. Then it was over, and Pedro was escorting her back to the place beneath the gallery.

'Go now, my love, hurry!' she begged him in great anxiety.

He sighed sorrowfully. 'The dance did not last long enough for me, my Francesca, but I will keep my promise.' His lips hovered over her hand. 'I love you, Francesca.'

'Please, Pedro, please hurry!' As her hand slipped from his, she said softly: 'And I love you.' Then she remembered, and whispered after him: 'Merry Christmas, Pedro, and her voice faded to nothing as he turned away and made towards the door.

The next moment she was staring horror-struck as the medallion fell to the floor from Pedro's pocket, and unknown to him! For a fraction of time Frances tried to move, to clutch at it from the floor before someone else did. But she could not move: she was suddenly paralysed with the sudden shock of seeing it fall.

She watched helplessly as a man's hand reached down and picked it up. The man held it out after Pedro's disappearing figure; then, on not attracting his attention, he started after him.

Frances saw him glance down idly at the object in his hand, then check his progress towards the door and look more closely at the medallion. She watched his expression change, and fear gripped her as he spoke to a companion and showed him the object.

The man who had picked the medallion up hurried from the room, leaving the second to work his way over towards where Sir Gerald and some of his guests were sat at the other side of the hall.

Frances, recovering a little from the shock of the incident, tried to think what to do. It was too late to warn Pedro now. He would be on his way back to the house already, no doubt unaware that he had dropped the medallion, and sure that he would be in the safe confines of Durville Court soon.

What of the man who had left the room shortly afterwards? He had obviously suspected something, and was probably following Pedro at that very moment. Why, oh why had Pedro carried the medallion that night?

Frances decided to find out what Sir Gerald was going to do. She made her way over, sick at heart towards his group. That which had been a private thing between herself and the Spaniard, a sign of the bond of love between them, now lay in Sir Gerald's hands for all to see. Her hopes of Pedro getting away unnoticed were now shattered. If only he had not come to the Ball. He had done it to be near her, but it had been a foolhardy action.

She could see her father threading his way over. She must persuade him to return to Durville Court quickly. She would feign illness, anything so that she might have a chance of warning the man she loved.

Sir Gerald was turning the medallion over, his lips a thin line. Then he said: 'It's a Don's, well enough. Could have been taken from a Spaniard, maybe a dead one.' He paused, then addressed the man who had brought it to him. 'Did you see this fellow's face?'

The man shook his head. 'No, he had his back to me, Sir Gerald.'

Sir Gerald pondered a while. 'You say someone's gone after him?'

'Yes, Captain Royce. He saw the man drop it.'

Sir Gerald said with a grim smile: 'This could be the rascal that escaped me last time. He has a liking for the district, it seems. If it is the rogue, then it's going to be the last bit of the world he'll see again. I'll have his head this time!'

Shortly afterwards, Frances, her parents and the escort were on their way back to Durville Court again, leaving the other guests unmasked and continuing to give a joyous welcome to Christmas Morning. She had had no need to feign illness. Sir Gerald's words, plus the shock of the incident had served to bring a swift change over her.

The bells from the village church sounding out across the white earth toiled peals of despair in her. Had Pedro got back safely? Had the man followed him to Durville Court?

When they arrived back at the house, John and Jesiah were waiting up to receive the family, and Frances learned in a muttered aside from John:

'Your Spaniard's abed, mistress. Gives his thanks to you, and he'll see you in the morning.'

Frances addressed him in an urgent whisper: 'Tell him quickly not to sleep tonight, and to get dressed quickly.' John's eyes narrowed questioningly, and she continued: 'He came to the Ball and dropped a medallion. It was found. I think that he was followed.'

She saw that her mother and father were eyeing her anxiously, and as John hurried away she went to stand beside them before the roaring fire, its flames leaping in crackling glee up the chimney. Its warmth seemed to revive her spirits a little.

'You are feeling better now, Frances?' asked her mother, gazing into her daughter's face.

'Yes, perhaps it was all the dancing. I was beginning to feel giddy, Mother.' She shrugged it off. 'All I need is a good night's sleep. I am very tired.'

Her father patted her affectionately on the

shoulder. 'In faith, you give me white hairs with these vapours of yours, my child.' His eyes brightened at a recollection, and he went on: 'Though you looked to be dancing uncommonly well in that last dance you performed.' Captain Durville then threw a glance at his wife, and turned again to Frances. 'Is that young man in favour with you?'

Her nerves were on edge, and she wanted nothing more than to go up to her room. She waved a hand in careless fashion. 'He dances well, but I know him only slightly.' Moving away from the fire, she planted a kiss upon Captain Durville's cheek. 'A Merry Christmas, Father.' Then she kissed her mother in turn on the forehead.

Her parents watched her climb the stairs slowly as if each step were an effort. As she disappeared from view, each of them was aware of the worried frown that had been on her brow.

About an hour later heavy knocking on the front door startled Frances in her bedroom, not yet undressed. For a moment it ceased, and she heard voices outside her window. She hurried to it and looked down. There were shadowy figures, and she could see the glint of metal. She opened the window a little. The voices floated up clearly. Orders were being given, and soldiers were spreading out along the rear of the house.

Just then she heard steps in the gallery and an urgent knock upon her door. John's voice called in a throaty whisper: 'Mistress Frances! Mistress Frances!'

She flung her door open. He stood there fully dressed, sword in hand, breathing hard. 'Soldiers, Mistress Frances. I told Pedro to stay aloft where he is. The house is surrounded.'

John hurried off downstairs, and Frances dashed to the gallery window. More soldiers! Some on foot, some on horseback, filling the courtyard. The house was indeed surrounded with them. She turned away, sick with fear.

At that moment her father appeared from his bedroom in night attire, a candelabra in one hand, and a sword in the other.

'Go back to your room, Frances, my child,' he ordered protectively on seeing her. Then he made quickly to join John.

'Father!' Such was the voice in which she called after him that he halted and turned to look back at her. He was shocked at the expression on her whitened face.

'My child, my child, have no fear, these are English soldiers. I have heard their voices.'

'There is no time. I must tell you... Oh, Father!' She plucked, then pulled him towards her room.

Downstairs, John was drawing the bolts. Captain Durville hesitated, then stepped inside the doorway, the candelabra he held aloft revealing the terrible distress expressed in his daughter's face.

Her words came urgently, the agony of her mind in her eyes for him to see plainly. 'Dear Father, have I not been a good daughter to you? Have I wronged you in any way?' His shake of the head had hardly begun before she went on: 'I have not sought after every man, never brought shame on your house.'

Puzzled alarm was in the bearded face that looked down on Frances. 'What is the matter? Why are you…?' Voices came from below. 'I must go,' he said, as he turned quickly to the door.

'No, wait, please, Father!' She clutched at his sword hand desperately. 'The soldiers, I know they are ours.' She jerked her head from side to side as if to rid herself of her fearful problem. 'Please help me, Father. I fear for what you will do. He is hidden, they are here to look for him. I did not seek it, he came. I know I have wronged you this once, but they would have killed him.'

Captain Durville gazed on her with bewildered anxiety. 'Fear of me? Hidden? Kill him?'

Her words were a broken whisper: 'I dared not tell you. He is a Spaniard.' She felt her father stiffen. 'He has been hidden these last months. Oh, please, Father, do not turn him over to the soldiers. He is my beloved. Love has come to me, Father, don't take it away from me. I will die.'

Wide-eyed disbelief was on Captain Durville's face. 'A Spaniard?'

'He was washed ashore, when you were away.' The tears fell down her upturned face. 'Please, please, don't let the soldiers take him. Let him live. If you think dearly of me, this one thing I ask of you in all my life.' Frances wanted to feel her father's arms comfortingly around her, to be told that all would be well, but the fact that his hands held sword and candelabra only served to emphasise the gulf between them.

For a few seconds they stared at each other, fear and misery etched on one face, stupefied amazement on the other.

Captain Durville seemed to age visibly in those seconds. He glanced towards the gallery and back to his daughter.

Frances searched his face desperately for hope. Then almost before she realised it her father was hurrying downstairs.

'Father!' she choked after him, and she clutched at the door for support.

A voice came clearly, good-humouredly,

from downstairs. 'Put up your sword, John Standard, this is English soldiery, not Spanish.' After a pause the speaker continued: 'Captain Lethgard of Sir Gerald's company. Forgive our visit at this time of the morning, Captain Durville. Sir Gerald sends his respects, and hopes you were not yet abed. But he thinks you have a Spanish visitor that you know not of.'

Frances stumbled to the gallery rail, to be joined by her mother.

'In this house?' her father said, seemingly astonished.

The soldier's voice came evenly: 'This medallion was dropped by a man at the Ball.'

'Yes, I was there. I heard about it.'

'The man was followed, and he was seen to enter this house,' the other said.

Frances's legs felt as if they would crumple under her. She heard the door slam to, and a stamping of feet. Weakly she watched as her father, grim-faced, preceded two soldiers into the hall below with John slowly bringing up the rear. The very thing she had dreaded for so long was now happening. Soldiers, helmeted, breast-plated and armed, were inside Durville Court and about to search for Pedro.

John lighted more candles at the request of Captain Durville, and then stood to one side while his master examined the medallion for a moment.

In the midst of her misery and fear, Frances felt sorry for John. Poor man, what was he thinking? No doubt he was regretting that he ever agreed to help hide Pedro.

'Now, Captain Durville,' said the senior of the soldiers, 'would you summon the rest of your household to be present here? If there is a Spaniard within these walls, they'll be safer with us.'

On hearing these words, Frances and her mother left the comfort of each other's arms, and walked slowly downstairs together to join Captain Durville, John, and the two soldiers.

When the household was assembled, Frances gazed about her in utter despair. The soldiers stood one on each side of the fireplace, their armour shining dully in its light, and looking menacingly tall in their helmets. Her father and mother stood between them, and the others in a rough half circle in front of them. She herself had drawn away from the fireplace to the edge of the group near the stairs. The light was not so revealing there.

John stood just offside her father, his face stern, giving no sign that he shared a secret with Frances. Flora stood next to him, grey hair awry, her face anxious. Next to her was Jesiah, rather bemused and not aware of the gravity of the situation.

At a distance from him stood Alice, struggling to place her hair in order under her black night coif. Casper, Elspeth and Mary were there, too, looking sleepy and bewildered.

Frances watched as Captain Lethgard held the medallion in front of them all. There was no way for Pedro to escape, not even to the cave. Soldiers surrounded the house. He was trapped!

She looked on helplessly as Captain Lethgard moved from one member of the household to another. She saw shakes of the head when he held the medallion out to them in turn. She tried to quiet by her will the thudding of her heart.

She began to tremble, felt the stool behind her legs and sank down upon it. She looked at the floor. The high boots stopped in front of her. The hand with the medallion was extended to her.

'Mistress Durville, have you seen this before?'

She glanced up at it and away, clasping her hands together quickly as if the touching of it would give her away. The hand pushed it nearer.

'Mistress Durville. Your answer.'

She tried to shake her head. It felt so heavy. Her mouth would emit no sound. Her mother saved her unknowingly.

'She has not been well, Captain, this night – even at the Ball.'

Frances found a whisper, a drawn-out sigh

of a sound and her tongue formed the word 'no'. She shook her head violently as if to make up for its lack of movement a moment ago, and she wafted the air with a hand as if to rid herself of any connection with the medallion.

Captain Durville hurried to his daughter's side, his face full of concern. Then he addressed Captain Lethgard, a note of anger in his voice. 'It is true, my daughter has been in some way sick these last weeks. We returned early from Sir Gerald's this night because of it.'

The other nodded understandingly, but without any change in the sternness of his features. His gaze switched from Frances to her father. 'I have to ask, Captain Durville. It is my duty. I am under orders from Sir Gerald.' He turned again to her. 'My hopes for an improvement in your health, Mistress Durville. I am sorry for any distress that has been caused to you.'

Frances raised her head and gave a weak smile. Her whole being was filled with a weary hopelessness. All vitality seemed to have drained away from her.

Captain Lethgard turned to the soldier who had accompanied him into the house. 'Two more men,' he ordered.

Within a minute the outer door opened and closed, and the soldiers entered, disturbing the warmth of the room and bringing with them a feel of the frosty cold outside. All eyes except those of Frances were on the soldiers.

'Now, Captain Durville,' Captain Lethgard said briskly, 'your permission to search the house.'

Frances trembled as her father hesitated. She knew the conflict present in his mind.

'There is no need. I will save you the trouble.' The voice with its foreign accent came clearly from the top of the stairs.

There, wood creaked in the shocked silence that ensued for a few seconds as everyone present riveted their eyes in that direction.

The steady deliberate steps descended, and Don Pedro de Ravallo appeared from the shadows. He came down the last few steps like a prince, dignified and calm, as if he were attending some great occasion in his own palace.

His voice, so unexpected, seared into Frances's brain, numbing her reasoning for a second. At the sight of him she jerked to her feet. His name was forced by her soul's anguish from her lips before she could stifle it, as she gazed horror-struck at him.

Suddenly, a slurring as swords left their scabbards swiftly.

'Wait!' rapped Captain Lethgard, seeing that the man on the stairs was unarmed.

'I am the man you seek – Don Pedro de Ravallo,' said Pedro, giving a small bow, and seemingly unperturbed at the bared steel facing him. He remained standing on the last step, so that he was raised above them all. He paid no attention to Frances, nor any heed to her cry of his name. Dimly she realised he must have entered the gallery by the door leading from the Standards' bedroom, and used often by John.

Her father could do nothing to help now. Captain Lethgard stepped forward, his eyes focused sharply on the Spaniard. 'You know Mistress Durville?'

Pedro turned slowly to regard the woman he loved, but his dark eyes appeared to look through her. No sign of recognition did he give as he gazed at her. He shrugged. 'No, I do not know this woman.'

Doubt showed in Captain Lethgard's face.

A smile curled in Pedro's mouth. 'But if heaven should grant me another life, I would wish to know her.'

'Are you the same who escaped us before?' asked the Captain, ignoring the gallantry coldly.

Pedro nodded.

'Where are the others who helped you escape?'

He shook his head slowly. 'There were only two. My friend died from wounds soon after.'

His questioner nodded in a satisfied way. Then he said: 'You speak English uncommonly well.'

'Are there not people in England who speak my language uncommonly well?' the Spaniard countered.

Frances's father, whose face had been contorted in worried thought the while, now screwed up his eyes and, frowning heavily, left her side and confronted him. 'Are you the rogue who dared to dance with my daughter a few hours ago? I perceive something familiar about you.'

Frances waited in terrible misery as Pedro turned a tired face to her father. 'You're well favoured with such a daughter, Señor. It would have given me great pleasure to dance with her, but,' he went on, giving a weary shake of the head, 'I was too weak for that. When a man is starving, food is the more important, even when beauty such as hers is set against it.'

Captain Durville turned away. For a fleeting moment sympathetic regret softened his face.

Frances's mind struggled against the nightmare taking place in front of her. The man she loved was giving his life away to take suspicion away from her and the household.

Captain Lethgard, his face merciless under the helmet, waved his sword. 'Take him outside,' he commanded.

Rough hands took hold of Don Pedro de Ravallo.

Frances threw herself forward. 'No! No!' she shrieked. She grasped at the leader's arm, half-kneeling. 'He has done nothing, please, please!'

Captain Lethgard hesitated momentarily. The soldiers paused, Pedro between them. The Captain looked down on her near-hysterical face. His eyes narrowed. 'This man says he does not know you, yet you are strangely concerned for his life!'

Precious seconds had been gained, precious seconds for her love. She seized them, nearly beside herself in fear for his life. 'It is Christmas Morn, Captain. Have mercy. Have we not been victorious over the Armada? This one man, can he do us any harm now? He has given himself over to you. I beg of you – do not kill him.'

The face above hers did not alter in its expression.

She tried a last desperate appeal. 'Let Sir Gerald decide.'

Just then her father hurried to her side, saying with great concern: 'Do not upset yourself so, Frances, my child. You are tired, overwrought. Tomorrow it will be forgotten.' Then, turning to Captain Lethgard, he went on: 'You understand, Captain, it has been a strain for us all. For some reason my daughter is highly strung these days. Take no notice of her behaviour.'

Frances turned aside, drained of all energy. Her father, heedless of her plea, it appeared, was sending the man she loved to his death. She saw the tension on Pedro's face as he waited.

Frances heard her father continue: 'Howbeit, while not wishing to deter you from your duty, Captain, I would counsel you on another aspect of the matter.'

Captain Lethgard, who had begun to

move towards the door, halted and turned to face Frances's father again. 'Oh, and what is that?' There was a note of impatient interest in his voice.

Captain Durville indicated Pedro. 'You will have observed that this prisoner is a man of education. He would not be a skivvy on his ship, but a man of some importance.'

'Perhaps that is true.' The Captain shrugged.

'Would not then Sir Gerald feel it important that this Spaniard gives us information? He may also be worth holding for ransom. And it may be,' added Frances's father, 'that he could tell of the disposition and patterns of Philip's other forces.'

Captain Lethgard frowned thoughtfully only for a few seconds, but a lifetime of agony for Frances. Not once did Pedro allow himself to look at her. Only the fire settling in its grate and the muffled sobs of the frightened maids broke the quiet.

John and Flora stood together, helpless, dismay on their faces at the turn of events.

Frances's mother, shocked into fear by her daughter's apparent disregard of the consequences of inviting suspicion upon herself, stared over her handkerchief at her.

Captain Lethgard studied the Spaniard standing impassively between his guards. Then his orders came: 'Tie him to the horse. Take him up to the Hall.'

Frances began to tremble, and put out her hand for support against the cold of the stone mullion as Pedro was pushed through the door into the passage. He gave a quick glance over his shoulder, and then was gone. Reprieved he was for a few more hours, but she knew he had gone to his death unless by some miracle a way of saving him could be found.

The household dispersed, shocked at the events that had taken place. Frances's mind was in a terrible confusion. Thoughts careered around it as if in a box with no opening. She wanted no talk with anyone, and stumbled blindly up the stairs. At that moment only one person mattered.

She gained her bedroom and shut the door behind her. She was helpless to aid Pedro. Christmas Morning, and her room a tomb of despair.

She heard the steps of her parents, dragging steps, as they went to bed. They hesitated outside her door, then moved away. Life stretched ahead for her, desolate, bare, with only memories. The man who gave them was gone.

What could she do? Minutes were precious. Rescue him again? Not this time. He was too heavily guarded and tied. But the seed of resolute courage had not finally died in her. Was this the way in which she showed her love for Pedro? a voice inside her hissed.

She scrambled to her feet, stumbled to the window and grasped the ledge until her fingertips hurt. Like a pealing of bells, one name came again and again into her mind. Queen Elizabeth! The Queen! The Queen! Guardian of England. Queen of all.

At any other time, Frances would have deemed her sudden plan stupid madness, a dangerous folly. But in her distraught state, nothing else was left. She would speak to the Queen, ask her mercy for Pedro. What was there to fear? She could not think of life without him. She had nothing to lose.

Strength was given to Frances from that moment. She flung on her heavy cloak with its enveloping hood, and tore at the hem of her dress to rid it of its impeding hoop. Then, uncaring whether she was heard or not, she flew down the stairs and out into the night.

Frances was away, galloping towards London. Had not Sir Gerald Colston said the Queen was at Richmond for Christmas? One thought only was in her mind: to reach the Queen and throw herself on her mercy. If the Queen would show none, then nothing would be lost. She, Frances, would die with him.

She must reach the Queen before Sir Gerald carried out the execution. She knew that Sir Gerald would show no mercy if Pedro was of no use to him, but she clung to the slight hope that he would delay execution until after Christmas Day. Perhaps even more time would be gained if he decided to find out if his prisoner was worth a ransom.

At times Frances almost fell off Bluebell's back through exhaustion. Daylight came, and the villages, countryside and deep-rutted byways, hard with frost and snow, merged into one for her. She was no longer conscious of individual things. By late afternoon she was almost falling from Bluebell through weakness, dozing off then awakening to the nightmare ride again. Only the love she bore for Don Pedro de Ravallo kept her hanging on to the horse's neck.

It was dark again when she reached the Thames. Bluebell was now reduced to a slow trot. Lights of boats along the river illuminated its surface like tiny glow-worms. Farther along explosions and coloured lights came from a great building. Fireworks! A million lights shone, it seemed, from its windows. Richmond Palace was in sight!

The display had finished when Frances reached the Palace, but the smoke and the smell of the powder lingered. She slipped from Bluebell and folded to her knees on the ground. She looked up at the figures ringing her with steel. 'I beg you,' she gasped weakly, 'to ask Her Majesty to grant me an audience. It is life or death concerning a Spaniard. Please.' She slumped forward, and the guards caught her as she collapsed. Frances's journey was over.

When she recovered consciousness, she found herself on a couch in a brightly lit room. There was talk and movement going on around her. She raised her head and immediately several women approached her.

'Where am I?' she asked of the nearest.

The woman smiled. 'In the Queen's Palace. You were brought in by the guards. We are Ladies in Waiting to Her Majesty.' The eyes about her regarded her with curiosity.

Memory returned, and rampant fear with it. Frances clutched at the speaker's wrist and said with terrible anxiety: 'The Queen, will she see me? Will she grant me an audience?'

The Lady in Waiting looked into the distraught face. 'Her Majesty is resting before the dancing until eight o'clock. She is not to be disturbed.' Then, seeing the look of stark hopelessness in the other's eyes she added: 'But your message will be given to her when she arises.'

Frances covered her face with her hands. 'There is little time!' Her voice faded to a whisper. 'There is little time. It may be too late.' She looked about her wildly, her teeth biting deep into her lip.

All around her was the hum and stir of a palace at Christmas where the Queen was in residence. Frances lay in utter dejected misery, insensible to the excited chatter of the Ladies in Waiting concerning the dance which was going on about her. A dozen times she asked the hour. She was given broth and a goblet of claret, and she was helped to tidy her appearance somewhat.

At last she was helped to her feet and escorted by two of the Ladies in Waiting from the room along a gallery, brilliantly lit by hundreds of candles in glass holders, towards a green velvet curtain behind which was a door. The curtain was pulled aside, and the door was opened into the Presence Chamber. Suddenly Frances felt frightened and weak of limb.

Unsteadily she entered with the Ladies in Waiting. She was aware of the women either side of her curtsying, and then she heard the door behind her being closed. She was left standing alone in the presence of Elizabeth, Queen of England. Trembling, dry-mouthed, feeling as if she would fall at any moment, she stood in awe of the one person who, with a word, could save Pedro.

There was a small beckoning movement of a hand, and green fire flashed from the royal fingers. Frances moved forward slowly until she was in front of the Queen, then dared to glance up at her.

'Are you recovered?' The voice was precise and light.

'Yes, Your Majesty.'

'We are told you have travelled far.'

'From Kilverton, Your Majesty.' Her hands

twisted together. How could she impress on her sovereign that every second was precious to Pedro's life? Perhaps it was too late already, and she was putting her own life in jeopardy for nothing.

'And you live in Kilverton?'

'At Durville Court, near Kilverton, Your Majesty.'

'Do your parents live?'

Frances nodded her head miserably. 'I live with my parents, Your Majesty.'

'You are unmarried?'

'Yes, Your Majesty,' she replied in an agony of impatient hopelessness.

For a moment a look of sad amusement appeared on the Queen's face. 'Then we are alike in that matter.' She went on: 'What business has your father, Mistress Durville?'

'He is a merchant trader, Your Majesty. He has two ships which have just finished in your service against the Armada.'

'Ah.' A look of satisfaction came to the Queen's eyes. 'England owes much to the likes of him.' Then fingers so slender and long that they made the rest of the hands seem small, pointed at some cushions on the steps of the dais. 'Be seated, Mistress Durville.'

Frances slumped on to the cushions with relief. Her legs would not have supported her much longer.

'Now tell us,' said the Queen, 'what is this thing that makes you travel the byways of England to see your Queen? It is said that you mentioned a Spaniard.'

The moment that Frances had waited for! The strange story spilled from her. Nothing was omitted. If her agitated manner clouded the narrative sometimes, her face told clearly what her words could not convey.

Towards the end her gaze slipped from the Queen. She dared not look at her for fear of what she may see on the royal face. At last she had told all. She covered her eyes with her hands and whispered a hoarse plea: 'I beg you for mercy on him, Your Majesty, though I fear he may be dead already.' The tears flowed between her fingers. 'I was so long in the coming to you.'

She was conscious that the Queen was moving. Then there was silence except for the distant murmur of voices outside the Presence Chamber. The die was cast – there was no taking back of her words.

The Queen's voice came matter-of-factly from behind Frances. 'You will be aware, Mistress Durville, that you have committed an act of treason?'

She nodded into her hands and whispered: 'Yes, Your Majesty.'

'And that the block is reserved for such offences?'

Frances's head bowed lower, a silent opening of her mouth her only answer.

'Yet even so,' went on the Queen, 'you would still seek a pardon for this Spaniard.'

All the agony and tension of the last three previous months was in the face that Frances turned and raised slowly towards her Queen. Even to form her words was an effort. 'If it would please Your Majesty.'

'Your choice of partner in this romantic

affair is unfortunate, Mistress Durville.' The Queen folded her arms, tapping one elbow restlessly with her fingers. Her voice had hardened with a note of contemptuous amusement in it. She continued: 'You have a brave heart, but we fear that your affections have rotted your brain.' She rounded on the bowed, kneeling figure in sudden anger. 'Are you of a mind that we have just driven that enemy from our very shores? By your own tongue you tell us your father fought for us. Now you ask for pardon for one of them. Is there not an Englishman that awakes your heart in all our realm?'

Frances remained bowed before the onslaught, her courage beginning to fail her. All was lost. The Queen of England was in anger against her!

She was aware of the Queen's movements about the room, the pull of a curtain edge, then the Monarch's figure in front of her again.

There was a sigh, and the Queen stated in calmer tones: 'The anchors of the heart drag deep, Mistress Durville.'

Frances dared hardly breathe, but looked unseeingly at the shimmering dress in front of her. Then she felt herself being helped to her feet by someone, and was dimly conscious of the Queen giving instructions.

Shortly afterwards the door closed on her as she lay on a strange bed. A terrible fear beset her now. She should have known better, Pedro was surely dead. Now she was to lose her own life.

Her mother and father – how she longed for them to come and take her back to Durville Court and its cosy confines. She would never see them again.

At last all the energy that had been needed to sustain her during her fight for Pedro's life was exhausted, and she cried bitterly.

Three days later, at two o'clock in the afternoon, she was taken before the Queen again. This time there was an older man as well, darkly dressed, and with a world-weary face. The Queen was dressed in ash-coloured velvet, with a rope of white pearls around her neck, from which hung a pendant of emeralds enclosing a huge diamond.

The Queen watched Frances as she approached. She observed the stiff curtsey and then the dulled eyes raised to hers afterwards. She said, not unkindly: 'We, too, Mistress Durville, have known what it is to languish in a strange place and not know one's fate.'

Then the Queen turned her head towards the door through which Frances had entered. She gave a command to the two gentlemen pensioners either side of it. They opened the door and a man entered the room to stand between them.

Frances followed the Queen's gaze. Don Pedro de Ravallo stood there! Their eyes met.

From afar Frances heard the Queen's voice. 'You have your father to thank for the stay of this man's execution. Sir Gerald halted it because your father thought your disappearance was connected with this man.'

Frances sank to her knees on a cushion, eyes wide and fixed on the figure of Pedro.

'Come forward, Don Pedro,' the Queen

commanded. She addressed him. 'Spaniard you may be, but a gallant man such as we like. You were willing to die rather than have harm come to this woman.' Then the Queen's eyes rested on Frances. 'And you risked your head to save his.' She paused, and her hands opened in a gesture to include them. 'Therefore, let it be witnessed that we grant a pardon to both.'

Uncontrollable joy filled Frances. Words she had thought she would never hear: a pardon! She found strength to stand upright on legs now weak from relief instead of fear. She glanced quickly at Pedro standing proud and dignified in front of the English Queen. Their hands touched for a moment.

He gave a small bow. 'Your Majesty has my million thanks for your mercy in victory,' he said. 'My country had not the advantage of such a fair and gracious queen.'

A small smile appeared on the Queen's white face, and a look of pleasure softened the watchful eyes. Then the eyelids dropped a moment and lifted again, and it was gone.

'Do you desire the hand of this woman?' she said briskly.

'If your Majesty pleases, above all.'

'It matters not to us – we want no part in marriage affairs.' An undertone of peevish irritability was in her voice. She waved a hand. 'But we would tell you, Don Pedro, that there is a price on all things in this world.' She paused and regarded him for a short while. 'And your pardon is not excepted from that.' Her eyes were extremely grave. 'Your price is that never shall you return, or attempt to return, to Spain. Nor shall you by any means communicate with any person in that country. If you go against us, you and those about you would be put to death in the way reserved for such cases. Nothing would save you.' The Queen finished speaking and observed him patiently. 'Your oath, Don Pedro,' she said after a few moments.

He turned slowly and looked into the face of his beloved, and she glimpsed a fleeting sadness behind the new-found happiness. This condition being demanded of him by the Queen was a further test of his love for Frances. He took hold of her hands in his and faced the Queen again.

'You have my word,' he said steadily and deliberately.

Neither Captain Durville nor his wife could have argued with their daughter's choice, once they knew that the match had been blessed by their Queen. Moreover, they came to be almost as fond of Pedro as Frances was.

For her part, Frances could not have been happier. She soon married the man she loved, and they had many, many happy years together.

And every now and again, either Frances or her husband would take his medallion out of the velvet-lined drawer where they kept it, and remember how it had brought them together. No matter how many costly and beautiful things they acquired together over the years, the medallion remained their most precious possession, for it symbolised their love, and the trials they had been through to win the right to their happiness.

The publishers hope that this book has given you enjoyable reading. Large Print Books are especially designed to be as easy to see and hold as possible. If you wish a complete list of our books please ask at your local library or write directly to:

Dales Large Print Books
Magna House, Long Preston,
Skipton, North Yorkshire.
BD23 4ND